THE HAUNTED PAINTING ON THE WALL

Devika A. Rosamund

Matador
9 Priory Business Park,
Wistow Road, Kibworth Beauchamp,
Leicestershire. LE8 0RX
Tel: 0116 279 2299
Email: books@troubador.co.uk
Web: www.troubador.co.uk/matador
Twitter: @matadorbooks

ISBN 978 1785893 711

British Library Cataloguing in Publication Data.
A catalogue record for this book is available from the British Library.

Printed and bound by CPI Group (UK) Ltd, Croydon, CR0 4YY
Typeset in 12pt Aldine401 BT by Troubador Publishing Ltd, Leicester, UK

Matador is an imprint of Troubador Publishing Ltd

MIX
Paper from
responsible sources
FSC® C013604

For Ava with love

CONTENTS

Chapter One

THE INVITATION

The invitation to stay at the haunted castle came on the second morning of the school summer holidays.

Tracy was running down the stairs, her shoulder-length, light brown hair flapping at her shoulders, just as the postman was dropping letters through the letter box. She ran to pick them up. There was a postcard from Spain for her mother, a letter from Worthing, probably from her grandmother, a couple of official looking letters, and one pale green envelope with a Scottish postmark. Nothing for Tracy. She placed the letters on the breakfast table for her mother to see when she came down.

Her elder brother, Sebastian, looked up from the computer game he was playing on his small laptop. He was wearing blue jeans and a purple T-shirt. He was two years older than Tracy and quite a bit taller. Tracy envied him for that and his blond hair.

"Why are you always so interested in the letters?"

he asked mischievously. "Don't you get emails from your friends?"

"It's perfectly normal to be interested in letters," replied Tracy with irritation. She knew he had seen her talking to a boy at the youth club a few evenings before. "Much better than being interested in your silly computer games."

Sebastian was about to answer her back when their mother came in and greeted them cheerfully, obviously anxious to stop a squabble that she saw might be about to start. She picked up the letters on the table and sitting down, opened them carefully one by one.

"What's that letter from Scotland?" asked Tracy seeing that her mother had put that particular green envelope to one side with a gasp.

"It's from your father's Great-Aunt Alice in the Highlands of Scotland," said her mother. "We haven't heard from her for years. She lives in an old remote castle in a forest in the middle of nowhere…"

Tracy looked over her mother's shoulder at the letter. She remembered her father talking about 'Aunt Alice's old haunted castle' as he had called it. He had said he loved the place when he stayed there as a boy. Tracy noticed that Sebastian also looked up with interest.

"Can you read the letter out?" asked Tracy.

Her mother sighed and started to read:

My Dear Tim and Catherine,

I do hope this letter finds your family all in good health. You may be aware that I have not written to you for some time due to my own poor health. I am sure, Tim, that you will not have forgotten me, your Great-Aunt Alice from Creag Castle in the Highlands of Scotland. I remember how you used to enjoy coming to stay here in your school summer holidays, years ago, with your brother. You loved searching for the ghost and the secret, long-lost hidden chamber in the castle. Of course, nobody ever found the chamber – it is just a legend.

Unfortunately, I have some very sad news. I have come upon hard times and will shortly have to sell Creag Castle and move away, as I can no longer afford the upkeep of it. My money was invested unwisely for me by an unscrupulous finance manager and it is lost. I am broken-hearted to have to leave my home, which has been in my family for so many generations, but there is no help for it.

As this is the last summer I shall be here, I should like to invite you and your two children, as my closest relations, to come and spend the school summer holidays here. It would give me great pleasure to see you again and to have some family members staying here for the last time. I am old, but my caretaker and housekeeper will look after you here. They have a son and daughter, Kevin and Beatrice, who are, I think,

*the same age as your two children, and will keep them
company. You may phone my housekeeper Marjorie
and let her know when you can come. I shall expect
you as soon as possible.*

Your loving Aunt Alice.

"Oh dear, your father will be upset about her
having to let the castle go," said Mrs Stewart. "What
a shame!" She hesitated, and then added, "But I do
hope she doesn't want to come and live with us!"

She put the letter down on the table and Tracy
grabbed it, as her mother went on: "We can't go and
stay with her in her castle. We have already arranged
to go to Spain this summer to stay with my sister in
her new house there, and your grandma is so looking
forward to coming with us."

Sebastian took a china bowl from the trolley and
helped himself to some Weetabix. "I'd really like to go
to that castle," he said. "It's surrounded by mountains.
Dad told us how spooky it is, and he and Uncle Ryan
used to enjoy making camps in the woods there."

"Yes…" cried Tracy, "it sounded wonderful the
way Dad talked about it. I'd love to stay somewhere
like that, and it will be for the last time."

"It's in a really remote part of Scotland," said
Mrs Stewart irritably. "I don't think you would like
it at all."

"We would like it, I know we would," said Tracy. She felt sure that her father would want to go there too, and she had high hopes of persuading him.

In the evening, Tracy was pleased to see that her brother obviously had the same idea. As soon as their father came through the front door, Sebastian brought up the subject of the letter from Scotland.

Tracy came running forward. "Mum doesn't want to go, but we want to," she pleaded. "You used to go there, didn't you?"

Her mother showed him the letter.

"That's very sad," he said. "I loved that rambling old place. I suppose it will be needing some renovation now and she can't afford it."

"We can't go and stay with her this summer," interrupted his wife.

"I know," answered their father. "We can't cancel our trip to Spain and disappoint your mother and sister, I realise that, but if Tracy and Sebastian are so keen on going to the castle, perhaps they can go alone. We might be able to pop up to Scotland for a weekend when we come back from Spain, just to see the castle for the last time."

Tracy was ecstatic and she noticed the excited look on her brother's face also.

Their mother looked worried.

"Oh, it would be all right," said their father. "Aunt Alice always had housekeepers and they were always very capable. The housekeeper will do all the cooking and laundry and her husband is the caretaker and gardener there. It would be safe enough."

Tracy was smiling in anticipation of the holiday. Suddenly her expression changed and she looked at her father nervously. "Is the castle really haunted?" she asked.

"Well, it's ghostly, but we never actually found the ghost ourselves…" said Dad hesitantly; then he laughed. "But the place has a reputation. There are some strange, old stories connected with the place that make it fascinating. One legend says that the castle has a dark side to it and that something very bad happened there long ago and that is why it is haunted. Another legend says that there is a secret chamber hidden somewhere in the walls of the castle, and that treasure is hidden there."

"How wonderful," said Tracy, clapping her hands. "If only we could find it, then Aunt Alice would be rich and she wouldn't have to sell the castle, would she?"

"I think if there really was a secret chamber with hidden treasure then somebody would have found it, by now, after all these years," said her father. "I am sure many people have searched for it, as your Uncle Ryan and I did during our holidays there. We searched all the walls in the whole castle from top to bottom for secret panelling."

"Well, we can search too," said Tracy. "We'll really try our hardest to find it."

"Yes, we certainly will," said Sebastian. "If that secret chamber and the treasure exists, I am going to find it!"

"If you can drag yourself away from your computer games!" said Tracy, watching her brother sorting out yet another game to play at the kitchen table.

Sebastian gave her a withering look and settled down to play it.

That night before Tracy went to bed, she looked at herself in the mirror. Behind her reflection, she saw her bedroom walls and her bed and all her books on the shelf. There was *Alice through the Looking Glass* that she was reading at school. "There is a whole world in there, through the looking glass," said Tracy to herself. "How magical it would be to step through the looking glass into that world as Alice did. My horoscope says something magical is going to happen, and I feel sure it will at the castle in Scotland."

★

Finally their mother agreed to telephone the housekeeper of the castle, and a date for their arrival in Scotland was agreed upon.

The two of them boarded the train at London

King's Cross Station for Inverness – it was to be a long journey of many hours. They both had window seats at a table, and Sebastian was happily playing computer games. He had two suitcases, one for his clothes and one for his laptop and games. Tracy was reading a book. As the train left the suburbs of London, the scenery became prettier.

"Do you think it will be very cold up there?" Tracy asked.

"Just a bit colder," replied Sebastian. "I have packed a lot of jerseys and jackets."

"Yes, so have I," said Tracy. "But it is summer. I hope we'll have some sunshine."

"Who knows?" remarked Sebastian absentmindedly, engrossed in his game.

"I love the idea of going on such a long journey and to such a magical place," said Tracy.

"So do I. Shut up and read your book," said Sebastian.

So Tracy shut up. She stared out of the window instead and watched the scenery become, what seemed to her, more and more mysterious – further and further from London, and everything that was familiar to her. She had never been to Scotland before and neither had Sebastian. They had never seen Aunt Alice before even though they had heard about her.

The journey took the whole day. It was early evening before the train pulled into the station at

Inverness. The train stopped with a jolt and Tracy and Sebastian pulled their suitcases down onto the platform. Tracy noticed that there was a chill in the air. Even though it was July, the evening air was cool – definitely cooler than it had been when they left London in the morning. This was Scotland, northern Scotland, and she imagined that it might be even colder in the Highlands, in the mountains. Tracy felt a shiver of excitement. She had a premonition that the two of them were about to embark on an adventure – good or bad she was not sure. She felt a tingle of fear.

Almost immediately, a tall, ruddy-faced man wearing a grey, tweed cap darted up to them. He introduced himself as Wilfred Jefferson, the caretaker of the castle. He was all smiles and greeted the boy and girl as if he was immensely pleased to see them. "Welcome to Scotland. I take it you are Sebastian and Tracy. Kevin and Beattie will be pleased to see you. They get lonely in the holidays up at the castle. I've got the car waiting outside the station to take you back."

The luggage was piled into the back of his van, and Tracy and Sebastian slumped back on the leather seats, tired after their journey. There was still a drive of one and a half hours to go. Their driver told them that he and his family lived in a fair-sized cottage in the grounds and that his wife Marjorie was the housekeeper; Sebastian and Tracy would be staying in the main house with Aunt Alice.

"Have you lived there long?" asked Sebastian.

"No, only two years," replied the caretaker. "We came up here from Derbyshire where I worked as a caretaker before. That family went abroad, so we took this job up here in the Highlands when it was advertised. We love the spectacular scenery here."

He paused and then added, "It looks as though we won't be here much longer though, as she is going to sell the place."

Tracy had dozed off. The journey had been long. She awoke with a jolt, and watched as the van travelled for miles on a road that was surrounded by a great forest mostly of birch and pine trees. It eventually turned on to a track leading through a great iron gate. The van swerved around a winding driveway lined with bushes, through wild-looking gardens leading up to the front door of a stone castle.

There were towers on each of the four sides of the castle and battlements along the lower level of the roof. The walls were of rough, grey stone and the front door was huge and wooden and shaped like a high arch. Some of the windows were built like slits, but not all of them – some were wide and dome-shaped with windows that looked as though they could be opened wide.

There was no moat or drawbridge, and Tracy was sure that Sebastian would be disappointed

about that, but the castle was fairly big and definitely seemed to have an aura of extreme mystery around it. She thought, at first sight, that it was a wonderful old building, like something out of a weird fairy story. The sun was shining and there was a feeling of cheerfulness about the place as though the castle was welcoming them. Tracy was pleased; she felt relieved. She stared at the huge old house in delight.

Then, the next moment, the sun unexpectedly went behind a cloud and the castle seemed to change its expression. All of a sudden, as it became clothed in shadows, Tracy became aware that now it no longer appeared cheery and friendly. It began to look hostile; it looked different. Tracy was startled.

Almost immediately, the sun came out again and the castle was smiling and happy once more. Tracy gasped. She wondered if she had imagined what she saw before – it was as though the castle had two faces – one good and one bad; as though it was hiding a dark secret. She shuddered.

Tracy tried to shrug the feeling off. She realised she didn't really want to stay in a haunted house – not now it was here, in front of her, in broad daylight. Yes, even though it was evening, it was still light. She remembered that summer evenings were long in northern Scotland. There were not so many hours of darkness as in the south.

"It's called Creag Castle," said Wilfred the caretaker. "Creag means rock or cliff in Gaelic. You can see how rocky the landscape is. The castle was built by one of your Aunt Alice's ancestors a few centuries ago. She never married and doesn't have any children herself."

After a few moments he added, "There are some lovely grounds around the castle. I am sure my son and daughter will delight in showing you around."

"Great," cried Tracy and Sebastian together.

"We are looking forward to meeting them," added Tracy politely. She looked up at the towers: there were four of them, all with pointed roofs. "Are those really shells that are embedded in the stone walls near the top of the towers?" she asked.

"Yes, those shells would have been put into the walls when the castle was first built, to ward off witches," said Wilfred. "That was a common practice in those days."

Sebastian laughed. "Did it work?" he asked.

"No, according to the local legends it didn't," replied Wilfred. Tracy noticed he turned away as if he regretted saying that. He then smiled and said cheerfully to them, "Well, here we are. I'm sure you'll enjoy your stay here."

The sun went behind a cloud again and a wind started to whistle through the branches of the trees above them. It felt to Tracy as though it was whistling a warning. She shivered.

Chapter Two

ARRIVAL AT THE CASTLE

Aunt Alice was at the door to meet them. She stood there smiling with her walking stick in hand. She was slightly bent, and looked delighted to see them; *a sweet but strong character*, thought Tracy, who prided herself on the belief that she was good at judging people's personalities.

Aunt Alice was fairly plump and wore a long, old-fashioned, dark grey dress pinned with an emerald-coloured brooch at the neck. She wore a kind of lacy bonnet on her grey locks of hair, which were bound up in a bun behind her head. Tracy thought she had only seen people wearing clothes like that in pictures of people in Victorian times! *Oh well, this part of the world is very cut-off, and Aunt Alice lives in an old castle*, she mused. This old lady suited the castle: a woman in modern clothes would not have looked right in this place.

Marjorie, the housekeeper, appeared at the door

behind Aunt Alice. She came out to welcome them – a much younger woman with short black curly hair, a rather drab, blue striped dress and an apron – it looked as if she had been cooking. Tracy thought she was dressed like an old-fashioned maid. There was damp flour on her hands and on her apron. She came forward to take their hands, but Sebastian pulled his away. Tracy tried to stifle a giggle. She knew he wouldn't want flour and water spilt on his computer case!

"I am so pleased you have come," said Aunt Alice. "Wilfred and Marjorie are my caretaker and my housekeeper."

"Well, how lovely it will be to have some more young voices up here," said Marjorie. "The castle needs more life in it, more people to fill it up, and we need the company. It gets lonely up here for all of us. There are no towns nearby. We are very glad to see you."

"So come on in," said Aunt Alice, beaming at them. "Dinner is nearly ready, isn't it Marjorie? You must be hungry after your journey. I do hope you'll enjoy it up here at the castle. Your father and his brother enjoyed themselves here so much in their holidays."

"Yes, I know they did," said Tracy politely.

A boy and girl, both dark haired, came running along the driveway at that moment. "Here are Kevin and Beattie to meet you," cried Marjorie. "Say hello to your new friends, Beattie."

"Ma, I don't need to be told that," replied Beattie with irritation. "I'm not a five-year-old. Do you think I'm not going to say hello? We've been waiting for them all day." She swung her ponytail back behind her shoulders.

"All right," muttered her mother. "Anyway, we're all going to eat together tonight in the big dining room, so you four can get to know each other."

"Yes, we will," replied Beattie, annoyed with her mother.

Kevin laughed. Tracy realised he thought it was funny. Her brother grinned. She wondered if they would get on with Kevin and Beattie. She felt sorry for Beattie and a little embarrassed, but she smiled.

"My mother always speaks to me like that and makes me look silly," said Beattie to Tracy as they were entering the large arched doorway.

"Never mind," said Tracy. "I expect she doesn't realise."

"Well, she ought to," replied Beattie.

The conversation was forgotten as they entered the well-lit hallway. The walls were of wooden panelling with attractive carvings of animals here and there. It was very unusual.

"Is there a secret passage hidden somewhere here behind these wooden panels?" asked Sebastian.

"I don't think so," said Kevin. "There is supposed to be a secret chamber hidden somewhere in the castle, but no one has ever found it."

"Yes, we've heard about that," replied Sebastian.

"Tomorrow we'll show you all around the place," said Kevin.

"With Aunt Alice's permission only," said his mother sharply. "You are not to do anything or go anywhere here without asking Aunt Alice's permission."

"Oh, they have my permission," said Aunt Alice smiling.

Tracy noticed that Marjorie looked stressed. The housekeeper put her hands on her hips as she said, "Aunt Alice, are you sure you don't mind them going around the whole house?"

Tracy was surprised that Marjorie also called her Aunt Alice. As if reading Tracy's mind, the old lady smiled and said, "I am Aunt Alice to everybody! Yes Marjorie, they are welcome to explore the whole castle." She turned to look at Beattie and Kevin, "But be careful of any broken steps or uneven floors in some parts of the castle, won't you?"

"And remember what I told you this morning, Kevin and Beattie," said Marjorie.

"Yes we will," shouted Beattie somewhat rudely to her mother, so that Tracy was a bit shocked. Then Beattie said more politely, "Aunt Alice, don't worry about us. We only want to help your great-niece and nephew have a happy time here, so we'll enjoy showing them around the castle and grounds tomorrow as you've given your permission." She pulled a face at her mother behind her back.

"That's very nice of you, dear," smiled Aunt Alice. "I am sure you and Kevin will be a wonderful support for them here."

"We will be," replied Beattie.

"We don't really need her support," muttered Sebastian to Tracy. "She's younger than us, I think, isn't she?"

"Shhh…" said Tracy to her brother. "She's only a year younger than me."

An angry look flashed across Beattie's face.

Tracy didn't want the housekeeper's children to turn against them as soon as they arrived. She looked at Beattie to try to think of something pleasant to say to her. "I like your silver necklace, it's very pretty," she said.

Beattie positively beamed at her. "Aunt Alice gave me this heart-shaped locket and chain for my birthday last year. It opens up, but I have not found anything to put inside it yet," she said. "Look, there's a rose flower engraved on the front of it, and the head and shoulders of an angel with wings on the back of it."

Just for a moment, a strange feeling came over

Tracy as she looked at the necklace. It was as if time stood still. She felt that there was something unusual about the necklace. Shrugging off the feeling, she said, "It's beautiful," and then added, "You know, we will need you to show us around tomorrow as we don't know anything about this castle."

Beattie nodded and smiled. Tracy was relieved. They followed the others in to dinner.

★

After eating the evening meal in what seemed to be an elaborately furnished dining room, they all, except Wilfred who had some work to do, went into a large lounge furnished with several velvet settees and comfortable armchairs. Even though it was July, there was a cheerful fire burning in the grate of a huge stone fireplace. On the walls were hanging some enormous oil paintings in gilt frames. Some were of scenery: the Scottish Highlands; some were of people dressed in old-fashioned costumes from long ago. There were women dressed in their finery; long, beautiful gowns; some of the men in the paintings wore kilts of brightly coloured tartan. A few were playing the bagpipes. Sebastian and Tracy looked around the room in wonder.

"Are these your ancestors, Aunt Alice?" asked Tracy. "Are they our ancestors too?"

"Yes, these are some of the people who lived here long ago," replied her great-great-aunt proudly, but Tracy noticed the sadness in her eyes too. Aunt Alice continued, "The castle belonged to my mother's family. She did not have any brothers or sisters so the house came to her. When she married, she and my father came to live here. My own brothers died in the war so the castle came to me."

"Can't you sell some of these paintings and make some money so that you can stay here?" asked Tracy suddenly. She immediately regretted saying that, in case Aunt Alice felt embarrassed.

"My dear," said Aunt Alice, "These paintings are not valuable. They were all painted by local Scottish artists at one time or another. Even if I were to sell them, they would not fetch much. Nothing that you see around you in the castle is of much value, unfortunately, even though I have it furnished nicely. The antiques that used to be here were all sold by my grandfather to pay off some debts that the family had accumulated."

"Who was the first owner?" asked Sebastian. "Was the castle built hundreds of years ago?"

"Yes, several hundred years ago," replied Aunt Alice. "I have a family tree. My grandmother's great, great, great, great, great, great-grandfather built it in the seventeenth century. He was a romantic and also an artist. He had two sons – one was a year older than the other. The elder one inherited it…"

"And the younger son was jealous," interrupted Beattie. "He did something very wicked in the castle."

"What was it?" asked Tracy. She noticed with surprise that Marjorie gave her daughter a warning look and Beattie looked away.

Aunt Alice smiled and seemed to pointedly change the subject. "Well," she said, "we'll all have some hot chocolate and biscuits now, and then Marjorie will show you your rooms. Your luggage has already been taken up. I am sure you are tired after your journey."

Marjorie disappeared out of the room to prepare the night cap for them all. When she had gone, Tracy leaned across to Beattie and whispered, "Was that something your mother didn't want you to tell us just now?"

"Oh, it's just a story about the two brothers," whispered back Beattie. "The castle is haunted. It's to do with them. It's rather an exciting story, really." She giggled. "I'll tell you and Sebastian about it tomorrow if you like. You're not frightened of things like that are you? It's only a story."

"Nuh-no…" stammered Tracy, looking out of the window at the increasing darkness outside as night set in.

Kevin frowned. He was sitting next to Tracy on the other side. He had been listening. "Yes, it's only a story," he said. "All old houses have stories attached to them. You don't have to take it seriously."

"Take what seriously?" Sebastian enquired in a rather loud voice. It seemed that he had only heard part of the conversation from where he was sitting on the other side of the room.

Aunt Alice looked up. She had dozed off for a few minutes.

"Nothing," replied Kevin quickly, answering Sebastian's question and eyeing Aunt Alice at the same time. Tracy took out a notepad and felt-tip pen from her bag and wrote in capital letters on it. She held it up behind Aunt Alice's back so that Sebastian could see it: THEY WILL TELL US THE GHOST STORY TOMORROW. She hoped that Aunt Alice, with her bad eyesight, would not see what she was doing.

Sebastian grinned. "Great," he said.

"Is the hot chocolate here?" asked Aunt Alice. At that moment Marjorie appeared with a huge jug of steaming hot chocolate and a tin of biscuits. Aunt Alice chatted amicably with her great-niece and nephew asking them about their home in London, and enquiring after the health of their mother and father.

★

Finally, as the grandfather clock in the hall chimed ten times, Marjorie stood up and collected the mugs and plates. "I'll show you to your rooms now," she said. "Aunt Alice told me to choose rooms for you on the same floor as her. I have made up the beds for you and made the rooms as cheerful as possible. I hope you will be comfortable."

"You must tell Marjorie if there is anything that you need," said Aunt Alice. "Is there enough cupboard space for them both in their rooms?"

"Yes, of course, Aunt Alice. I have kitted the rooms out completely for them. Wilfred has fetched wardrobes and chests of drawers from the other rooms for them, and I have hung up curtains. We have spent a lot of time making the rooms comfortable and attractive for them."

Aunt Alice nodded appreciatively. "Well, I'll leave you to take them up then," she said, "and I'll see you both in the morning for breakfast at nine o'clock. Marjorie will show you where to go and where is the nearest bathroom."

Aunt Alice gathered up her shawl and made to go out of the room.

"Kevin and Beattie, you can go back to our cottage now," said their mother, looking especially at Beattie. "It's getting late and time for bed."

"Oh really?" remarked Beattie in mock surprise. "I would never have known it."

Kevin looked at his sister and stifled a laugh. Tracy glanced at her brother and was sure that he and Kevin were going to get on well – they were the same age and seemed to have the same sense of humour – they both liked to laugh at their sisters!

They all left the lounge together. The fire was dying down and Marjorie switched on the hall light. Kevin and Beattie went out by a side door, and Marjorie led Sebastian and Tracy to the foot of an enormous winding staircase with ornamental wooden posts and a rail going up.

The hall light was not very bright. Tracy looked up the huge staircase. There seemed to be shadows everywhere. There was an eerie feeling about the stairs as if someone was lurking in the shadows waiting for them. Tracy shuddered.

Chapter Three

A GHOSTLY EXPERIENCE IN THE NIGHT

"Your bedrooms are on the first floor," said Marjorie. The stairs were carpeted, but the wooden boards creaked loudly as they went up. The landing above them was pitch black. Marjorie went first and switched on the light. Again, it was not very bright. A long corridor stretched in front of them with many doors on either side. She walked several metres along it and pointed to a door painted blue and white. "That is Aunt Alice's bedroom," said Marjorie. All the other doors around them seemed to be beige in colour. Then she walked past a couple of other doors and turned the handle of a door on the same side.

"This room will be your bedroom, Sebastian," she said. Sebastian came forward eagerly. The door opened into a fairly large room with white walls.

There were bookshelves full of books, a wardrobe and cupboards, a desk with a chair and a large bed in the middle of the room. On the wall was a painting of an old-fashioned steam train passing through some mountain scenery. Sebastian looked at it: "Nice picture," he remarked.

"Yes, I thought you'd like that," said Marjorie. Then she added, "There is a bathroom on the other side of the corridor. You both can use it." She opened the door of the bathroom to show them.

They left Sebastian in his room. Marjorie led Tracy to another door along the corridor on the same side as Sebastian's room. When she opened the door, Tracy gasped with pleasure. It was obvious that Marjorie (and Wilfred as well, she supposed) had gone to a lot of trouble to make the room attractive for her. It was very much a girl's bedroom. There was a pink flowery duvet on the bed with rose-coloured pillow cases. On the dressing table were an ornamental mirror and a pretty brush and comb set. There was a shelf with a vase of flowers and books, and another shelf with dolls from various countries in national costumes, probably part of a collection.

On the wall was an enormous painting of the castle surrounded by its immediate gardens, in a gilt frame. It looked as though it had been painted a long time ago, when perhaps the castle was new. The picture seemed to literally shine out of the wall as if it was the most important object there. Tracy noticed it immediately.

"Wow, look at that picture!" cried Tracy. "It's this castle. What a beautiful painting of it. How bright and cheerful the castle looks. It lights up the whole room, doesn't it? Did you choose this room for me because of that picture and the other things here?"

"Oh no," said Marjorie. "I chose this room because of the lovely view from the window. Wilfred and I have brought all the furniture here from storage. I chose the duvet and bed sheets and everything else. I discovered all these things in other parts of the house. I found that picture hidden away in one of the rooms and I thought how perfect it would look on your wall."

"Thank you very much for taking so much trouble," said Tracy. "I am longing to see the view from the window in the morning."

"It looks out over the lawns and bushes in the front of the house, and across the forest to the mountains," said Marjorie. "You are at the front of the house as you see it in that painting."

Tracy began to open her suitcase.

"I'll leave you now," said Marjorie. "You remember where the bathroom is, don't you? I'll see you in the morning. I'll be up to make breakfast for you and Aunt Alice at nine o'clock. You'll see Kevin and Beattie after that."

"Thank you," said Tracy politely, "and good night."

Marjorie left the room and Tracy could hear her going down the huge staircase one step at a time. She was left alone, and in spite of the prettiness of the room Tracy felt a shiver of fear. She wondered if it was because of what Beattie had said in the lounge about ghosts. Tracy wished she had not told her that just before they were going to bed on their first night.

She searched in her suitcase for her nightdress and her washbag. She was about to go out and find the bathroom when she looked up; she could not help noticing the painting on the wall, again. It was truly fascinating and seemed to glow in the electric light of the room. The castle looked wonderful in the picture – *As it still is*, thought Tracy. *It looks a happy place. Not a house to be afraid of at all. I really have nothing to fear.* She comforted herself with the thought. "This picture will help me realise that the castle is not haunted," she said to herself. "I'll look at it if ever I get scared in this big house, and then I'll see that I am being foolish."

Tracy picked up the fluffy white towels left out for her, found the bathroom and washed and brushed her teeth. She was sure that her brother had already gone to bed or perhaps he was playing his computer games! Anyway, she wasn't going to go in to him now. She went back into her room, put on her bedside lamp and got into bed.

For a while she lay there under the covers thinking about the events of the day. There were a few blankets on the bed as well as the duvet. It was cold in Scotland, but Tracy was snug. She was tired and quite soon she turned the lamp off and fell into a dreamless sleep.

★

It was night. Suddenly Tracy awoke with a jolt. Something had disturbed her in her sleep. There seemed to be the sound of someone crying in the distance. A feeling of panic came over Tracy; for a moment she didn't know where she was. Everything around her was pitch black. Then she remembered – she was in bed in a room in the castle in Scotland. She was alone. Sebastian was in another room and Aunt Alice was in another, but who was that crying? It sounded like a young girl. It could not be Aunt Alice and it definitely was not her brother. It seemed to come from somewhere else – perhaps another part of the house. Who else was in the castle?

A wave of fear came over her as she began to see shadows in the room as her eyes got used to the darkness. The moonlight was shining through the window. The curtains were slightly open. Quickly,

Tracy switched on the lamp next to her bed. At once the crying stopped. Had it been her imagination, she wondered?

There was no crying now. Perhaps she had dreamt it? She looked around the room in the light of the bedside lamp. Her eye caught the painting on the wall, and then she jumped in surprise. Somehow the painting looked different, but she couldn't put her finger on how it looked different. It wasn't quite the same, but she wasn't sure how. The castle in the picture no longer looked bright and cheerful as it had done when she first saw it. It looked gloomy and shadowy, and Tracy couldn't help thinking it was a little bit sinister-looking. Oh dear, she didn't like it as she was seeing it now.

Oh, it must be because it's night, thought Tracy. *This bedside lamp is not so bright, and the shadows in the room make the picture look grey. It makes it look as though the castle is standing there in the night!*

She tried to laugh at herself, but her laughter felt hollow. She managed to cheer herself up by thinking about the story of the hidden treasure in the lost, secret chamber, somewhere in the castle. They were going to search for it soon. How wonderful if they could find it.

Tracy looked at her clock. It showed that it was three o'clock in the morning. She kept the bedside lamp on and turned away from the picture. She heard the sound of someone crying again, and she even thought she heard the sound of a man laughing. Tracy dived deeper into the bedclothes. Soon she fell asleep again, and did not wake up until the sun's early morning rays shone through her window.

Chapter Four

A DISCUSSION
IN THE
TREE HOUSE

Tracy was so glad when she saw it was morning. Her clock showed that it was eight o'clock – *good*, she had time for a shower before breakfast. She collected the clothes she was going to wear: some brown corduroy trousers, a green top and a sweater. Probably they would be going into the woods sometime today.

She glanced up at the painting on the wall. It looked normal again – bright and cheerful as it had last evening – just as beautiful. *Of course it does*, thought Tracy. *The room was so shadowy last night even with the light on, and I was probably half asleep anyway – that was why the picture looked different.*

She washed and dressed and went out into the hall. On a sudden whim she knocked on her brother's door. He didn't open it, but she thought she could hear him moving inside. She knocked again and he came to the door.

"Oh, it's you," he said. "I've been up awhile." He had a pile of computer discs on the table and he had obviously been playing the games.

"I've finished playing this computer game," said Sebastian, "otherwise I wouldn't have opened the door." He grinned.

"It's breakfast time," said Tracy. "Shall we go down? Did you sleep well?"

"Yes I did, actually," replied Sebastian. "I was very tired. Did you?"

"Yes…" hesitated Tracy. "Did you hear anything in the night?"

"No, I was asleep – only the wind in the trees before I nodded off. Why? Did you? Did you hear any ghosts wailing in the night? It's disappointing… I didn't." He laughed.

"Wouldn't you be afraid if you did have an experience like that?" asked Tracy, annoyed at him for making so light of the subject.

"No, I think I'd rather like it," said Sebastian. "It would be something to tell the boys at school in September."

"Don't wish for things like that," said Tracy. "It's not a good idea."

Sebastian laughed out loud. "Are you really

frightened here?" he said. "You had better stop it or you will start imagining things."

"I thought I heard someone crying in the night," said Tracy. "I knew it wasn't you or Aunt Alice. Someone was crying."

"There's no one else in the house," replied Sebastian.

"Well, I did hear something," said Tracy. "And I also thought I heard a man laughing. It wasn't very nice."

"I'm sure you were dreaming. I'm not afraid of anything here," said Sebastian. "This is a wonderful place, exactly as Dad said it was."

Tracy nodded as if she wasn't sure. Sebastian came out and they both went down the staircase to the breakfast room.

★

The breakfast room was next door to the lounge where they had sat last night. It was obvious which room it was as they could smell porridge, and eggs and toast cooking. The large room was also a kitchen with a fair-sized oak table and chairs around it. There was a stone slab floor, which had obviously been scrubbed.

Aunt Alice was sitting by the fireside in a comfortable armchair. A small fire had been lit in the grate as it had been in the lounge last night. Marjorie was standing at the stove – a wonderful old Aga.

"Lovely to see you nice and early," said Marjorie. It was ten minutes to nine. "Sit down and choose which cereal you would like. Or would you like porridge?"

"I would like porridge," said Tracy. "This is Scotland and I want to eat what you eat in Scotland. Porridge is typically Scottish, isn't it?"

"Yes it is," replied Marjorie. "What about you, Sebastian?"

Sebastian looked at the boxes of cereal on the shelf. "I'll have Weetabix," he replied.

"He always has that," said Tracy.

Aunt Alice sat down at the big, old table. Marjorie spooned porridge in a china bowl for her, and handed her the jug of cream and the honey pot.

"Did you two sleep well?" Aunt Alice asked.

"Very well," replied Sebastian.

"Yes, very well..." said Tracy.

Sebastian grinned at her. "Tracy heard noises in the night," he said.

"No, I didn't," replied Tracy angrily. She didn't want him telling them that.

Marjorie looked at her questioningly. "Did you wake up in the night, dear?" she asked. "The wind was quite fierce last night."

"Yes, that's what it was," said Tracy, glaring at Sebastian. "But I slept well after that."

"I hear nothing at night, because I don't have

my hearing aids in," chuckled Aunt Alice. "I usually only put them in at meal times, to talk to Marjorie… and now you are here. But if I don't answer you at other times, you will know that I can't hear you."

Tracy wondered why Aunt Alice didn't put her hearing aids in all the time.

"The hearing aids are uncomfortable for her," remarked Marjorie, as if reading Tracy's mind. "They are old-fashioned ones, and rather bulky."

At that moment, Kevin and Beattie came through the door. They were both wearing jeans, and Kevin wore an olive-green sweater with bright orange monkeys knitted into it. Sebastian stared at him and raised his eyebrows.

"Did you wipe your feet when you came in?" asked Marjorie.

"You always ask us that – and yes we did," said Beattie irritably.

"Well, it can be muddy out there," said her mother.

"Do you always wear sweaters like that?" Sebastian asked Kevin.

"Mum knitted it for him," giggled Beattie before her brother could reply.

"It's quite chilly today," said Marjorie. "Your jacket and other sweaters are in the wash. You can't go out in shirtsleeves."

Kevin rolled his eyes. "Anything for peace these

days," he said, and grinned. Tracy thought he looked handsome anyway in spite of the awful sweater!

The next moment Marjorie ushered her son and daughter out of the room, saying she wanted to tell them something before they went out. Sebastian and Tracy heard Beattie's irritated voice in the hallway, "Yes, you've already told us that. We know you don't want us telling them the ghost story."

They all came back in the kitchen again, and Kevin and Beattie sat down at the table. They both raised their eyebrows across at Sebastian and Tracy. Tracy pretended she hadn't heard anything.

"Would you like to have some breakfast with us?" asked Aunt Alice.

"No, they've already had breakfast at home, Aunt Alice," replied their mother.

"Well, pour them some orange juice then, dear," Aunt Alice insisted.

★

It was a lovely sunny day, though a little windy. Aunt Alice pulled her shawl around her and leaned closer to the fire. "I always have a fire lit even in summer," she said. "It gets chilly up here in the Highlands."

"Yes, of course you do," said Marjorie. "I light it for you in any of the rooms where you like to sit."

"Are you coming outside, then?" said Kevin.

"We'll show you the grounds and the woods first as the sun is shining now. You never know when the weather might change up here. It could be raining or stormy later."

Their mother nodded in approval. "Don't go too far into the forest, you could get lost. It goes on for miles you know."

"We are aware of that," said Beattie. Her mother sighed and turned away.

The four of them, led by Kevin and Beattie, left by a back door. Kevin led them all around the outside of the castle. Even though it was sunny, it was quite cold outside and the air was very fresh. There were large rocks protruding from the ground and they could see high mountains peaked with snow. The scenery was really spectacular. The forest seemed to stretch out on all sides of the castle behind the grounds, which were quite big in themselves. There were lawns and some flower beds, but it was all rather overgrown. "It's rather a large garden for one gardener to deal with on his own," remarked Sebastian to Kevin.

"Yes, there are no other people working here," replied Kevin. "I like gardening and sometimes in the holidays I help. I have created a vegetable garden at the bottom."

Tracy was impressed. Kevin went up in her estimation. She felt him to be a tolerant, good natured boy. "He isn't always on his computer like you Sebastian. He has some other interests!" she said, laughing.

"Shut up, Tracy," said Sebastian, "I'm not on the computer right now, am I?"

"No, but…" began Tracy.

"Do you two always argue?" asked Beattie. "I had hoped we could all be friends here."

"Don't you and Kevin ever argue?" said Tracy, annoyed.

"Yes, all the time," replied Kevin. He grimaced and walked ahead, taking Sebastian with him. "Beattie never stops chattering on. She's too much sometimes!" he said to Sebastian.

Sebastian laughed.

"Wait for us, you two," shouted Beattie, trying to catch up with them.

The next moment they arrived at the cottage where the Jefferson family lived. It was a very pretty stone building with a slate roof and a small garden of its own around it. There was also a pond with water lilies; a few ducks were swimming there. Beattie ran into their house to fetch some chocolate and a bottle of lemonade.

"We'll take you a little way into the forest after you've seen the grounds that belong to the castle," said Kevin. "There's a gate and a path near the sundial at the bottom of this lawn that leads into the forest. We'll keep to the path and show you a tree house that we've made. We have a rope ladder attached to a branch and you can climb up."

Sebastian gave an exclamation of pleasure.

"There is also a little old summerhouse nearby where we go sometimes," said Beattie. "We'll show you that another time. We sometimes have picnics there."

There were mostly fir trees in the forest, but a few other large old deciduous trees had managed to take root here and there – perhaps planted long ago. They all went along a narrow path for about one hundred metres and suddenly came upon a sprawling old oak tree which, although protected to some extent by the pine trees all around it, looked as though it had become twisted and bent through the years in the fierce Highland wind. There were many knotted and gnarled branches, high and low on the tree.

"Here's the rope ladder," said Kevin. It was hanging from a branch just as he had described; they all climbed up, one by one. A small wooden house made from planks and shaped like a shed, was perched on some branches above their heads. It swayed slightly in the wind.

"It's very safely secured," said Beattie. "Our dad made it for us."

"Yes, he's very clever at making things," replied Kevin. "That's why he's a good caretaker. I helped in building it too."

"It's fantastic," said Tracy, in admiration. Sebastian nodded.

Inside the tiny house was a rather dusty rug on the wooden boards of the floor, and cushions all around. There were also several warm woollen blankets. Beattie handed the blankets out to the others as they sat down on the cushions.

"It's cosy up here," she said. "You just have to wrap yourself in a blanket against the wind that comes through. The roof has polythene, but we couldn't stay up here in a storm." She got out the chocolate and took some plastic cups off a shelf. She poured out some lemonade for all of them.

"Now you can tell us the story of the brothers and the ghost," said Sebastian. "We want to know everything about the castle. We want to search for the secret chamber."

Kevin grinned. Beattie giggled. "Mum said we can't tell you the ghost story," she said.

"That's ridiculous," said Sebastian. "Your mum is a bit of a fusspot isn't she? Whyever are you not allowed to tell us?"

"Mum thinks it's too frightening," said Beattie. "She threatened us last night and this morning too, that if we tell you the ghost story and what happened years ago, she'll stop our pocket money."

"Oh, for goodness sake," said Sebastian. "We wouldn't tell her you've told us, would we, Tracy? Now you've mentioned the ghost, you've got to tell us about it. And you've whetted our appetites more now by making it such a mystery."

"I don't think we'd better tell you. Mum is already annoyed with Beattie," said Kevin.

"Is it really that scary that your mum thinks it would frighten us so much?" said Sebastian, getting worked up. "Is that it? We are not small children, as you said yourself to her, Beattie, yesterday. Now I really want to hear the story. Don't you think it would make us more nervous thinking that something awful happened here and we don't know what it is?"

"Yes, that's true," interrupted Tracy. "If something terrible happened here, then I want to know what it is, otherwise I shall lie awake all night wondering about it."

"Oh dear," said Beattie, "I never should have let on that there was something." She giggled.

"Well, you did," said Sebastian annoyed, "so that's the end of it. And now you have done, you will have to tell us the rest. Tracy's already scared, aren't you, Trace?"

"No, I'm not," snapped Tracy. Then she turned her head away, somehow giving herself away. "But I would like to hear the story or I won't be able to sleep now, as I said before."

Kevin glanced at her. Tracy saw an understanding look in his eyes.

"All right, I'll tell you both the story," said Kevin, "but you must not let Mum or Aunt Alice know that I have told you. Do you promise that?"

"Yes, we do…" said Sebastian and Tracy together.

Chapter Five

THE STORY
OF THE TWO
BROTHERS

"The story is," began Kevin, "that the man who had this castle built long ago was a Duke. He had two sons – one was only a year older than the other. When their father died, he left the castle and also his possessions to his eldest son, but nothing at all to the younger son. It was customary in Scotland for the eldest son to inherit the property, but the younger son was resentful. Also, he was friendly with his father's enemies. His father and elder brother were royalists who supported the King.

"The younger son did not get on with his father in life and he became very bitter against his elder brother. After their father's death, the elder son who was married, invited his younger brother to stay here, to live here with him and his wife. The younger brother schemed to ruin him. He wanted to kill him and his wife too. He went a bit crazy. He began to study dark magic and witchcraft.

"He wanted to put a curse on the castle so that it would burn down. He tried all kinds of dark, magical rituals here in the castle, secretly, at night. He tried to call up evil spirits, ogres, witches and devils to destroy the castle… He even tried to set fire to the castle himself one night, but luckily he did not manage it.

"He set up all kinds of things in the rituals. He used a cauldron to mix magical potions to make spells," went on Kevin. "He set up statues of devils and witches and collected things for his ceremonies. He used ghastly ingredients like dried blood and the bones and skulls of dead animals. He stored these things in the house. However, in spite of all his dark magical practices, nothing happened – the castle remained safe, his brother remained safe. None of the rituals or spells worked."

"What happened to the younger brother in the end?" asked Sebastian.

"He went mad," said Kevin, "and then he killed himself. Then they found all the things he had used in the rituals, and they knew what he'd been doing."

"Did he kill himself here?" asked Sebastian.

"He might have done. I'm not sure," replied Kevin. "This much about the history of Creag Castle is written in a book of local legends of castles in the Highlands. No one even knows if it is really true.

Mum thinks the story would frighten you and spoil your holiday here and that's why she has forbidden us to tell you."

"That *is* a frightening story," said Tracy. "Perhaps the younger son is the ghost, a really horrible ghost. But what about the treasure hidden in a secret chamber in the castle? We have heard about that. Do you think the ghost could be guarding the treasure? Perhaps he doesn't want anybody to find it."

"That is another legend," said Kevin. "It is just an old story that has passed through the centuries, that there is a secret chamber somewhere in the castle where treasure is hidden. It is probably an old wives' tale."

"It's all quite exciting, I think," said Beattie. "I'm not afraid of ghosts."

"You don't have to sleep up at the castle at night," said Tracy. She shuddered as she remembered her ghostly experiences in the night. "Dark magic is dangerous. I'm not sure if I really want to stay here."

"Magic isn't real, so don't be silly, Tracy," said her brother. "I'm not afraid either and I feel insulted that Marjorie is treating us like children. After all, we could have read about these legends in a book, and the people that lived here long ago are our ancestors. We need to know about the history of the place. Try to grow up, Tracy."

Tears pricked Tracy's eyes.

"And if you left now, then Mum would know we have told you something, and we would be in trouble," said Beattie. "So please don't let on."

"No, please don't," said Kevin.

"No, I won't," muttered Tracy, almost inaudibly.

"You'd better not, Tracy," said Sebastian, "or you'll be in trouble with me!" He put on a really fierce look.

Tracy turned her head away.

"I'd like to do a tour of the whole castle from the inside this afternoon, to get a feel of the place," said Sebastian. "I want to search for this secret chamber."

"Beattie and I have searched for the chamber so many times," said Kevin. "We have examined all the walls, and probably everyone who has ever stayed here has. It is probably only a legend. However, I am happy to search again with you."

"So am I," said Beattie joyfully. "We'll put all our effort into it."

"Of course we need all the help we can get if we want to have the remotest chance of finding the secret chamber," said Tracy.

"Okay, right," said Sebastian. "We'll begin after lunch."

★

Around one o'clock they made their way back to the castle. Lunch was served in another downstairs dining room which they were told was called the lunch room. There was a huge polished rosewood table and some old-fashioned looking furniture. On the walls were more old oil paintings of Scottish scenery.

"I like to use the rooms downstairs," said a smiling Aunt Alice when they were sitting down at the table. "It is such a waste to live in a castle and not use the rooms. There are so many rooms upstairs that we don't use, that we have no use for."

After lunch Wilfred went back to his work outside. He had a workshop in a garage at the back of the house. He was a man skilled at all trades. He was adept at plumbing, electronics, carpentry, gardening and all kinds of craftwork – anything that was needed in the house.

In the afternoon it was raining. Aunt Alice said it was all right for them to stay in the castle and explore it. Once again Marjorie took her son and daughter out of the room to speak to them. They could hear Beattie protesting to her mother. Sebastian raised his eyebrows.

When they came back in, Aunt Alice turned sympathetically towards Beattie. "My dear, don't mind your mother telling you things. She is an excellent housekeeper to me – the very best. She feels responsible for the castle and for all of you, but I know you will be careful and won't go up on the roof or do anything dangerous."

"Thank you, Aunt Alice," said Beattie. She glared at her mother.

Tracy felt disturbed, but strangely comforted by Aunt Alice for seeming to be such a solid, reassuring presence amongst them all. She was happy to let them explore the whole castle and she trusted them. Tracy decided that she liked her and remembered that her own father had praised her. Her calm, cheerful character made Tracy feel safe suddenly. *If Aunt Alice could live here alone and not feel afraid, even though obviously she knew the ghost story, then perhaps,* thought Tracy, *she need not be afraid of staying here either.* She pondered on it.

"We'll start on this floor," said Kevin leading the way as they left the lunch room later. There were many doors set in the long corridors of the castle and two wooden staircases – the large elaborate one that they had been using, and a smaller staircase at the back of the house which looked as though it might have been used by servants long ago. They went along all the corridors and into the rooms. Everywhere they went, they examined the stone walls, prodding and banging on them, in case there was a place that suggested a hidden door. Many of the rooms were almost bare, but some of them had old furniture and ornaments stored in them, sewing and linen baskets, trinkets and old-fashioned wash basins.

They climbed up the steps of the towers at the four corners of the castle. They passed each floor on the way. When they reached the fourth floor of one of the towers, Kevin stepped out into the corridor.

"This floor can only be reached by the tower steps that we have just climbed," he said. "The other staircases only go up as far as the third floor."

"If only we could find the hidden chamber," said Beattie for the hundredth time. "Why would it have been kept hidden?"

"Perhaps it was originally a priest hole," suggested Sebastian. "We were learning about priest holes at school in our history lessons. They were secret rooms in big houses where Roman Catholic priests hid during the Reformation period, when England was supposed to be Protestant. Priests had to hide or they were arrested."

"But we are in Scotland," said Kevin. "Mary Queen of Scots was Catholic, and what about the Stuarts?"

"I bet it wasn't a priest hole. I bet it was a secret room for hiding their treasure," said Beattie.

"If it exists at all," said Sebastian. "We can only hope."

★

After they had explored the inside of the castle, Kevin led them outside. "I'll show you the underground cellar," he said. "There is an entrance to it at the back of the castle."

It was not easy to get through the overgrown bushes and brambles that covered the stone entrance to the cellar in the castle wall at the back. Finally, they found some broken steps leading downwards into darkness. There was no door to the cellar. It looked as though there had been one once but the wood had partly rotted and then partly been carried away, perhaps for firewood in a cold winter long ago.

There were only about six steps leading underground into a dark basement area with a low ceiling. There was a bad smell down there of rotting and decay. Tracy wondered if some small animals had died down there. It was quite horrible. The stone slab floor was completely uneven and Sebastian nearly lost his footing. They could just about make out that ahead of them was a large basement which housed some old, heavy looking furniture.

"We will need to bring torches down here if we want to explore properly," said Kevin. "There's no point in going down here now without light."

They emerged back out of the cellar into the open air.

"There are so many secrets about this castle,"

said Beattie. "We are really cut off here in this lonely place away from civilisation."

"Where do you go to school?" asked Tracy.

"We are weekly boarders," replied Kevin. "We board for five days, and on Friday nights Mum and Dad fetch us in the car to spend the weekends back here at the castle, and then we go back to school on Sunday night or early Monday morning. It's an hour's drive away."

"And Mum and Dad do the weekly shopping when they pick us up for the weekend," said Beattie. "They only go to the town once a week. That shows you just how far away we are from civilisation."

Kevin laughed. "We are not that cut off," he said. "It's only twenty minutes' drive to the nearest village."

"Far enough," murmured Tracy. She had a feeling also that the castle was hiding secrets. She hoped they were not going to prove to be too unpleasant.

Chapter Six

THE BOOK IN
THE LIBRARY

At last it was teatime and they all, except Wilfred
who was working somewhere in the grounds, went
down at four o'clock to join Aunt Alice in yet another
room on the ground floor. This was the tea room –
very pretty and cosy with another fire burning in the
grate and a small tea table laid with a white-starched
embroidered tea cloth, plates of scones and jam,
cakes and biscuits. There was a large teapot covered
with a brightly coloured tea cosy.

Aunt Alice started to pick up the teapot to pour
the tea into the cups for them, but Marjorie rushed
up and took it from her. "Oh, let me do that for you.
The teapot is rather heavy."

"Thank you, my dear," said Aunt Alice. "I
thought I could do it, but I will be happy to let you
do the honours for us."

Marjorie cut one of the large cakes into slices
and offered them all a piece.

"We are very lucky that Aunt Alice is inviting us to meals and tea here too, now that her great-niece and nephew are here," she said, and looked especially at Beattie. "I hope you have expressed your thanks to her."

"Of course we have," replied Beattie irritably. "Anyway, thank you Aunt Alice."

Aunt Alice smiled. "It is my pleasure," she said. "It's so lovely to have young voices in the house again. Now you are on your school holidays we can all enjoy meals together. It's such a long time since we have had such a cheerful table to eat at. I want to experience again, for the last time, some of the warmth and gaiety that these castle walls have known in the past. It was a happy house, you know."

Tracy sat up and beamed. She was so glad Aunt Alice said that.

Beattie smirked. She was careful not to let her mother or Aunt Alice see. Kevin grinned.

Sebastian opened his mouth to question the old lady, but then thought better of it. He felt certain she was not going to answer any questions of his about the ghost story and, anyway, he knew he must not let on that he knew anything about it.

After tea, Marjorie bustled her son and daughter out saying they had something to do at home for a couple of hours. "They can come back when I serve the supper tonight," she said, without asking them.

It was still raining hard. Aunt Alice suggested that Tracy and Sebastian go into the library to look at the books.

"There are some lovely old children's books with pictures in there," she said. "You can spend an interesting couple of hours in there until dinner time."

★

The time passed quickly, for there were little stepladders in the library, and Sebastian and Tracy were able to climb up and bring books down from the higher shelves to look at. Many of them were very old and contained colourful, original illustrations protected by tissue paper. There were old-fashioned fairy-tale books and books about dragons and sea monsters in the children's section.

"I've had enough of looking at children's books," said Sebastian. He went to another part of the library and climbed up the tallest stepladder to look at some books on the very highest shelf in the library. It was very dusty and cobwebby up there. He reached up and pulled some old books off the top shelf, releasing a cloud of dust in the air in front of his face. He coughed violently. The books were quite heavy. He carried them down and carefully placed them on the table.

"It looks as though nobody has cleaned those shelves for years," said Tracy. "There is so much dust. We had better make sure we put all the books back properly or Aunt Alice and Marjorie will be annoyed with us."

Sebastian wasn't listening. He was opening the books, one by one, and reading the titles.

"I am hoping I might find an old book about Creag Castle with information about the location of the secret chamber," he said. "I suppose we could come back in here every day and search the whole library."

"And probably find nothing…" said Tracy sadly. "If it was written about in a book, surely people would have found the hidden chamber years ago."

Sebastian climbed up the ladder to put the books back. "There is nothing here on this top shelf about Creag Castle," he said. "These are all historical books up here about the wars between England and Scottish clans years ago."

As he reached up and forcefully banged the heavy books back into place on the top shelf where he had found them, suddenly there was a loud click and scraping noise as though the books had hit against something and caused some damage on the shelf.

"Oh, no," gasped Tracy. "Whatever have you done now, Sebastian? Have you broken something up there?"

Sebastian groaned and stepped onto the highest rung of the ladder. He peered over the edge of the dusty wooden shelf and pulled out the books again to see what damage he had done to the wall at the back. Suddenly he cried out in amazement.

"There's a cavity in the wood up here at the back of the shelf which has just opened up!" he said. "I must have banged something with the books. A space has clicked open, and there is something hidden inside it!"

Another cloud of dust flew out as Sebastian put his hand inside the hole and brought out a much smaller ancient-looking book which looked as though it was falling apart. The cover was of thin leather, but it was broken. Sebastian carefully carried the book down the ladder. He placed it on the table and opened it. The pages were yellow with age and some of them were loose. The book came apart in his hand.

"I do believe this is a book of estate plans of the castle," said Sebastian excitedly. "Look at this! Somebody has hidden it in that secret cavity on the top shelf behind the books!"

Tracy came over to look. The two of them leaned over the book and slowly turned the pages. There were plans of the inside of the castle on every page showing all the rooms and corridors, and also of the gardens around it as they once had been. They could also see the tower rooms and the attic.

"And look, there is the cellar underneath the castle," said Tracy, as they turned another page, "and what is that pathway leading diagonally upwards from there to a small room next to the tower there?"

Sebastian leant forward and let out a cry of triumph. "That's it!" he shouted. "It must be! Look, it's a passageway that we definitely have not seen when we were exploring the castle. It's a secret passageway, surely!"

They both stared at it.

"And that small room next to the tower… what room is that?" whispered Tracy. She was not sure why she was whispering.

"There is no small room like that joined onto any of the towers that we have seen," said Sebastian. "That could be the secret chamber with the treasure! What a find! This is amazing. This is our lucky day."

"Is that the tower at the front of the castle on the left side?" said Tracy.

"It looks like it," answered Sebastian. "Listen Tracy, we'll not tell any of the adults about this yet. This will be our secret for now. We've already investigated the walls of the towers quite thoroughly and not found any openings there, so we must go back down the cellar again and search for the entrance to the secret passage."

"How wonderful it would be if we could find it and get up to the secret chamber and find the treasure!" said Tracy. "So it really might exist after all!"

"We hope so," said Sebastian. "I am going to make a copy of the map on this page. We can't carry this book around. It's so old and the paper might crumble." He took a sheet of paper from another table, and a pen from his pocket. Carefully he copied the map of the inside of the castle onto a clean sheet.

"There are some words written inside the secret chamber on the plan," said Sebastian. "They are so small, I need a magnifying glass to read them."

Tracy opened the drawer of a desk nearby and found a magnifying glass. She handed it to her brother and looked over his shoulder at the map he was copying.

"These words here are written by hand in ink," said Sebastian. "The ink has turned brown with age and the words are a different colour to the print. Can you see?"

Tracy leaned over the map again to have a look.

"It says *chamber of witchcraft*," said Sebastian.

Tracy gasped.

"Remember the story that Kevin told us," said Sebastian. "It looks like this might have been the room where the youngest son of the Duke was practising dark magic. Perhaps it was kept secret because of that. A few centuries ago it was a criminal offence to practise witchcraft. Perhaps they did not want anybody to find out about it."

"Ooh," said Tracy. "It's a bit scary."

"I don't believe in magic," said Sebastian scornfully, "and Kevin told us that the magic spells he tried to conjure up to destroy the castle didn't work anyway. But this discovery is incredibly exciting."

"But this is not the chamber where the treasure is hidden, surely," said Tracy. "Perhaps there is another secret room."

They scanned the pages of the book, but there were no more passages like that leading to any other chambers anywhere in the castle. Sebastian had counted the rooms when they were exploring, and those they had seen were all accounted for on the plans. On other pages of the book, the passageway from the cellar and the small chamber were not there at all. Only on one page were they included, which seemed to indicate that they were not to be seen by everyone.

"This is definitely a secret chamber," said Sebastian, "even if it *was* used, at one time, for the practice of witchcraft by the Duke's son."

At that moment they heard the dinner bell. Sebastian carefully closed the ancient book. He climbed up the stepladder with it and placed it in the cavity at the back of the top shelf. He put the other larger, heavy old books in front of the hole to keep it hidden, as it was before. He climbed down the stepladder and moved it away to another part of the room, so that nobody would guess they had been in that part of the library. He and Tracy left the library and made their way to the dining room.

★

Kevin and Beattie were already there. Tracy was anxious to tell them about their discovery, but it was obvious that there would be no chance to talk to them privately that evening or show them the map. Wilfred was sitting at the top of the table and Aunt Alice at the other end. Marjorie was serving the food. They all sat down to the hot dinner that Marjorie had made for them. After a dessert of apple charlotte and cream, they went to sit in the lounge to drink hot chocolate until it was time for bed.

The grandfather clock in the hall chimed nine times. Marjorie collected the mugs and took them to the kitchen. Then she led her family to the door. "We'll be off now," she said. "See you tomorrow."

Sebastian called out to Kevin as they left. "Tomorrow you can come to my room and I'll show you my computer games."

"I like computer games too," said Beattie.

"I'll show you another time," muttered Sebastian.

Tracy stared at her brother. She guessed that he wanted to tell Kevin about the map and was not bothered about letting Beattie in on the secret. Tracy was annoyed. She decided she would talk to him about it in the morning.

"See you tomorrow then," said Kevin, as he and Beattie left by the back door.

As Aunt Alice fumbled about looking for her walking stick by her chair, Tracy watched as Sebastian took the map out of his pocket and fingered it. Nothing was going to stop her brother in his search for that secret passage. She knew he would find it and it was going to lead to the chamber of witchcraft. Tracy had a feeling that there was something unlucky about it.

Chapter Seven

THE MYSTERIOUS PAINTING

Tracy and Sebastian sat with Aunt Alice for five minutes longer.

"Have you had a nice day?" she asked kindly.

"Wonderful," answered Tracy. "The castle is an amazing place."

"Yes, I have always loved it," said Aunt Alice. "I think everyone does who comes here. I wish I had invited you and your family here before, but I was so unwell for quite a few years and I did not feel like entertaining."

"It's nice to know that you are feeling better now, Aunt Alice," said Tracy politely, "but so sad that you have to sell this beautiful castle."

The old lady got up and moved around the room switching off the lamps on the wall.

"Have you got everything you need?" she asked. "Has Marjorie furnished your rooms nicely?"

"Oh yes, beautifully," replied Tracy. "Hasn't she Sebastian?"

"Yes, wonderfully well," replied Sebastian rather absentmindedly, still feeling the map in his pocket. He yawned.

"Well, you are tired," said his great-aunt. "We must all go to bed. I am tired too." She gathered up her shawl and her walking stick.

Aunt Alice switched on the hall lights. Tracy and Sebastian followed her up the great stairway. Again, it creaked as they went up. Tracy realised that she had not noticed it creaking in the daytime when they went up, *but of course*, she thought, *in the daylight you don't notice things like that*. They all went to their rooms and shut the doors behind them.

Tracy put on all the lights in her room – she wanted to banish all the shadows. She changed into her nightdress. It was soft, pink cotton with a frill around the neck. She went to brush her teeth and have a quick wash, and then came back to the room.

She had avoided looking at the painting, but now she went up close to it and had a good look at it. The castle looked beautiful as though it was cheerful in sunlight. Yes, she saw that there was a sun in the sky peeping out behind a cloud. There was a peacock-blue sky. At the front of the castle some of the front garden had been painted with bushes and trees. It did not look much different from how it looked now, but Tracy was sure that the painting was very old. There was the drive leading up to the front door, where they had come yesterday.

Tracy moved away from the picture, turned off the main light and got into bed. For quite a while she kept her bedside lamp on, but when she became sleepier, she turned that off too. It had stopped raining now and the moon was, again, shining in through the window as it had the night before so that it gave some light in the room. It was shadowy. Tracy gave a shudder as she remembered the map and the hidden chamber of witchcraft. Now that it was night, she was not quite sure whether she really wanted to go up that secret passage after all. It all sounded rather frightening. However, she was tired and soon fell asleep.

★

It was, again, in the middle of the night that Tracy woke up. This time she was not sure what had awoken her. She saw the moonlight shining through the window creating shadows on the walls. Then she heard it.

It was that sound of crying again – a girl crying. The sound was coming from somewhere in the house, she was sure. She sat up in bed and switched on the bedside lamp, but this time the sound of crying did not stop. Then she got a shock.

The picture on the wall seemed to be all aglow, but it was an unnatural light that shone from it – or was it the effect of the moonlight? Tracy got out of bed. She was determined not to be afraid. She went nearer to the painting. Then a shiver passed down her spine. Something had changed in the picture again. Something was different, she knew. It was definitely not the cheerful painting she saw in the day – the castle looked gloomy and sinister again – *very* sinister, she thought. Then she saw it – there was no sun in the picture, the sky was not a peacock-blue anymore, it was more like navy blue; there was the same cloud she had seen before, but behind it – she could not believe it – there was a moon! Yes, it was a moon, not the sun.

Tracy pinched herself to see if she was dreaming. Surely she must be dreaming.

"I don't like this picture," she said to herself, "but no, I can't ask them to take it away – think how offended Marjorie would be, and perhaps Aunt Alice would be upset – and what could I say? That I am afraid of the picture? Then they might think that Beattie and Kevin have been telling us ghost stories and that is why I am nervous – then they might get into trouble."

She pulled herself together and moved closer to the picture, hoping to see it differently – surely her eyes were deceiving her. The sound of crying had stopped – it started and then it stopped again. Tracy could not take her eyes away from the picture. Suddenly, she saw that there was a girl's face looking out of one of the upstairs windows of the castle in the picture. She had not noticed it before. The girl seemed to be leaning out of the window – she seemed to move. She was dressed in pink, the same colour as Tracy's own nightdress. A feeling of horror came over her as she suddenly felt sure that the sound of crying had come from that girl.

Tracy gasped in terror and then ran to put on the main light. The crying had stopped, but the castle in the painting still looked the same: gloomy and sinister and cast in shadows. The girl was still leaning out of the window, but seemed to be still now, and the moon was still shining behind that one cloud, making everything shadowy. It was night in the picture.

Tracy ran in great fear back to her bed. She turned away from the picture and pulled the covers over her. This must be a dream and she must fall back to sleep and dream about something else. It was a horrible dream.

She lay there for a long time under the covers and did not turn towards the picture. She fancied she heard the crying again for a while, and she was sure that she heard a man's laugh, as she had done the night before. The laugh seemed to come from somewhere else in the castle. Tracy sank deeper down into the bed. Eventually she fell into an exhausted slumber and slept until morning.

★

Sunlight was shining through her window as Tracy opened her eyes and sighed with utter relief. She did not feel afraid during the day. In the day everything looked bright and normal. If only the nights didn't have to come. She jumped out of bed and instinctively ran towards the picture to look at it. It was, again, the cheerful painting of the castle in sunlight. The sun was shining behind a cloud. There even seemed to be a few painted flowers in the gardens. Tracy wondered why she hadn't noticed them before. She gazed up at the windows. There was no girl leaning out of the window. The windows were blank. Nobody there.

Tracy wondered for a moment if she was going mad. Was it all her imagination? Was it because she had been made so nervous with the idea of ghosts and witchcraft in the castle that she was imagining things in the night?

Tracy went into the bathroom to have a shower. When she was dressed she stopped outside her brother's room and listened; then she knocked.

"Is it you again, Trace?" Sebastian called out. Tracy turned the door handle and peeped inside. She saw that Sebastian was sorting out his computer games as usual.

"You are not really going to play games with Kevin, are you?" asked Tracy, incredulous.

"It's an excuse to get him alone to show him the map," said Sebastian.

"I guessed that, but what about Beattie?" protested Tracy. "Aren't we going to show her too?"

"I'd like to talk to Kevin about it privately," said her brother. "Perhaps he might know something else that he hasn't told us yet."

"I don't think so, and that's very unfair," said Tracy. "We can all be included in making plans for searching for the passage in the map. We can all study the map together and discuss it. Let's all meet together in the tree house and Beattie can see the map too."

"All right," said Sebastian reluctantly. "I am just afraid that she might open her big mouth and tell her mother or Aunt Alice about it."

"Of course she won't, if we tell her not to," said Tracy impatiently. "She's not that stupid, and you can't keep it from her. She will find out we are searching and then be more likely to tell somebody about it out of revenge, if we don't let her in on the secret."

"Yes, I suppose you're right," said Sebastian. "I'll tell Kevin that we'll all meet in the tree house at ten o'clock then. You can bring Beattie there."

Tracy was pleased, but she had come to

Sebastian's room to speak to him about something else. She looked around nervously and hesitated.

"Oh, Sebastian, I want to tell you something…" she began.

"Can it wait until later?" said Sebastian. "Let's get down to breakfast. I'm hungry."

"No please, I want to tell you now," pleaded Tracy. "I had a dreadful experience in the night."

Sebastian looked up, curious. "What was it?" he asked.

"Well…" hesitated Tracy. "Come into my room. I want to show you something."

Sebastian made a sound which sounded like exasperation, but he followed Tracy into her room.

"You see that painting…" Tracy began.

"Yes, it's a painting of this castle," said Sebastian. "It's a marvellous painting, but I bet it was done a long time ago."

"Well…" said Tracy. She didn't quite know how to go on. "In the night that castle changes."

"Whatever do you mean?" asked Sebastian.

"It's a castle in the day now," said Tracy, "in the sunlight… And at night it is a castle in the night. There is a moon shining in the sky and the castle is gloomy and all in shadows, and I saw a girl's face looking out of the window. Also, I heard crying."

Sebastian looked at the painting more closely, and then laughed out loud.

"Don't be ridiculous," he said. "Are you imagining things? Are you so frightened when you go to bed that you start seeing things that aren't there? That's not funny, Tracy. You had better pull yourself together. If the housekeeper or Aunt Alice think you are afraid here because someone has told you the ghost story, then you could get Kevin and Beattie into trouble."

"I know that," sobbed Tracy. "But I'm afraid of the picture. I really did see those things."

"No you didn't," shouted Sebastian almost too loudly. "Just drop these ideas. You were dreaming, and you have to know the difference between dream and reality."

Tracy dried her eyes on her sleeve. "I'll try," she promised. "Perhaps I was dreaming."

"Yes, you most definitely were," said Sebastian. "We are going to search for the secret passage today. Perhaps you had better not be involved with it if it's all making you so nervous."

"No, I want to be part of it," whimpered Tracy.

"Then let's go down to breakfast," said Sebastian firmly.

★

When they got down to the breakfast room Marjorie was there. "I thought I heard someone shouting," she said. "Was it one of you?"

71

"It was Sebastian shouting for me to get up," answered Tracy quickly. "I wasn't ready."

"Oh well, there's no need to shout," said Marjorie. "I don't mind if you are a few minutes late."

Aunt Alice was sitting in the armchair. She had just put her hearing aids in. "I didn't hear them," she said smiling. "That's the best thing about not being able to hear. You always get a good night's sleep."

They all sat down to breakfast.

"Did you sleep well?" enquired Aunt Alice.

"Very well," answered Sebastian and kicked Tracy under the table. Tracy kicked him back.

"Yes, I also slept very well," said Tracy.

"Too well, it sounds like, if you overslept," said Aunt Alice. "Well, I'm glad you are comfortable at night."

After breakfast, Beattie and Kevin came over. Today Kevin was wearing a grey jacket with a plain navy jumper underneath. Obviously they were out of the wash! He looked happier.

"We'd like to meet with you both in the tree house," said Tracy before her brother could say anything. "We've got something to show you."

"What is it?" asked Beattie.

"I'll tell you on the way there," said Tracy, eyeing Marjorie.

Beattie noticed the look and followed Tracy out

of the room quickly. Sebastian and Kevin also came outside. Tracy knew her brother would tell Kevin on the way to the tree house, as well.

Beattie was very excited when she heard about their find in the library. "Whoopee! A secret passage that will lead us to the secret chamber and the treasure," she said.

"I'm not so sure," said Tracy. "I have a very bad feeling about it."

Chapter Eight

DOWN IN THE CELLAR

The girls were already sitting inside the tree house waiting, when the boys arrived.

"I have heard there is a map," said Beattie, excitedly.

Sebastian took out the folded map from his pocket and spread it on the floor of the tree house. They all sat on the cushions and leaned over the map to study it. Beattie immediately found the secret passage and the chamber on the plan and pointed to them enthusiastically. "But what are these words next to the chamber?" she asked.

"*Chamber of witchcraft,*" said Tracy, shuddering. "That's what somebody wrote in pen and ink on the page in the book."

Kevin gasped. "Perhaps that was where the Duke's youngest son was practising witchcraft," he said.

"Yes, that's what we think," said Sebastian. "If

only we could find the entrance to the secret passage which leads up to it. According to this map, the passage starts down in the cellar. I hope we can find it. The walls of the castle are of such thick stone."

"It has been hidden for so long probably," said Kevin. "I don't think it's going to be easy to find. Dad has been down there so many times and he certainly has never found it. Aunt Alice also does not know about it and she has been living here for years!"

"We'll do everything we can to find it," sang out Beattie, "and it will be our secret until we do. Then they will be thrilled if we find the treasure."

"There's no mention of treasure," said Sebastian impatiently. "It's a chamber of witchcraft! We don't know what we might find. But let's get going."

"I'm not a bit afraid," said Beattie ceremoniously. Kevin raised his eyebrows. Then Beattie added, "We'll ask Mum to make us a packed lunch, then we can carry on searching all afternoon without interruption."

"That's a great idea," said Sebastian. Beattie beamed at him in surprise – it was the first time he had praised her.

"I'll go and ask Mum now," she said, jumping up and climbing down the stepladder. They watched from the tree house as she ran back to the castle. Ten minutes later she was walking back with a heavy picnic basket under her arm.

"Mum thinks we are going to have a picnic in the summerhouse," said Beattie giggling. "I didn't tell her we are going down the cellar."

"I'll need to go back to the cottage and get torches," said Kevin. "We'll have to move some of the old furniture stored inside the cellar so that we can get to the walls."

Kevin went back to their cottage to look for torches. Sebastian and Tracy also had one each in their rooms and they fetched them. The four of them then met outside the tool shed in the grounds and helped themselves to some garden forks and other tools with which they could probe the stone walls in the cellar.

"Dad won't mind us borrowing these," said Kevin. "He likes me using them in the garden sometimes." He led the way to the back of the castle, towards the overgrown bushes and brambles that covered the stone entrance to the cellar in the castle wall. They went down the broken steps as they had done the day before, and switched on their torches. Again, the horrible smell of rotting and decay hit them.

"I don't think this cellar has been used much except by animals," said Beattie in disgust. "No wonder nobody found the entrance to the secret passage!"

They all shone their torches into the cellar and could now see clearly the filth and dirt which had collected in that damp, underground basement and which covered the heavy wooden tables and chairs, pots and pans, china basins and vases – objects similar to those stored in the empty rooms of the castle upstairs, only in much worse condition. There were also many old wooden barrels lying around on the ground.

Sebastian stepped forward. "The map seems to show that the passage starts somewhere near the top end of the cellar on the left," he said. They all began to make their way there, and as they did so, they were surprised to find an archway hidden in the corner leading into another basement area – another room.

"We didn't know this was here," said Kevin in surprise. "We looked in here a couple of times before and were sure the room didn't lead anywhere else. I expect Dad knows about it though."

There were one or two broken steps leading down into the second room. That too was full of dusty, large old pieces of furniture and wooden barrels. They shone their torches around, but there was nothing that looked like the opening of a passage.

"We'll move some of this old, heavy furniture away from the walls if we can," said Sebastian. "Then we'll have more chance of seeing if there is another opening somewhere behind."

It was not easy though. The wooden furniture looked as though it was made of solid oak. It was very heavy and had obviously been there for a long time. All four of them tried together to heave the heavy pieces away. They were finding it impossible.

"Let's shine our torches into the gaps between the furniture," suggested Kevin, "and we can also, perhaps, get under this table and press our hands between these chairs to feel the wall, and see if there are any gaps in it."

They managed to move some smaller wooden pieces away from the wall, but found nothing. Beattie went out of the cellar and fetched some cloths and a bucket of water so that they could wash the stones of the wall, and examine them better as they explored them.

Kevin took one of the garden forks, and began to prise into the gaps and cracks of the stones in the walls all around the two cellar rooms to see if there were any stones which might give way. Sebastian took another tool and did the same. They spent a long time searching.

"I really don't think there is an entrance here," said Sebastian disappointed, after they had been investigating the walls all around the basement area for more than an hour. "Let's have our picnic lunch now and then we can go on searching afterwards."

They all made their way back through the two

cellar rooms and out into the open air. It was breezy outside. They sat down under some tall pine trees and opened the picnic basket. There was a rolled-up plastic tablecloth inside and they spread it out on the grass. Tracy set out the plastic plates and Beattie poured some lemonade into the cups. Kevin lifted out the cheese sandwiches and divided them up between them. Sebastian retrieved some apples and opened two large bags of crisps. For the next half hour they ate and chatted.

After their picnic lunch the weather looked as though it was beginning to change. Dark clouds began gathering in the sky.

"Let's get back to work now," said Sebastian.

Quickly they packed up the picnic basket and made their way back to the entrance of the cellar. They pushed their way through the bushes, going down the cellar steps again into the two basement rooms. For the next couple of hours they explored every nook and cranny of the walls that they could reach. They were on the point of giving up when suddenly Beattie screamed.

"What on earth's the matter?" asked Kevin.

"Something hairy brushed my face and went down my neck," screeched Beattie again.

"Look, there it is," said Tracy pointing her torch. "A long-legged hairy spider. It's running away there."

They all looked down and shone their torches

on it. The spider ran over to a corner of the room. As they watched it, they saw a mouse dart out from behind a piece of furniture and run in the same direction. It seemed to disappear into the ground. Following it, Kevin cried out in surprise. "It really has disappeared into the floor here," he said. "There is a small hole beneath the stones and rubble. I am going to try to dig them away with this garden spade."

Sebastian came over to help and they found that the whole floor in that spot was covered with loose stones and rubble. They worked for a while and managed to dig and sweep the stones away; then they saw that in that area the stone slabs underneath were smaller and shaped differently into a pattern.

At last, the pattern of small stone slabs beneath the rubble was laid bare, and it was obvious that some of the stones were loose and not joined to the others. The girls came over to try to help in shifting the stones in the pattern. They managed to move some of them and slide them out. Some caked mud fell away and a gap was revealed underneath with stone steps going down – more broken stone steps. They cleared more stones away.

"This is amazing, but is this the passage in the map? Why is it going downwards?" asked Kevin.

Sebastian shone his torch down the steps. "There are only about six steps here," he said. He climbed carefully down the steps and saw a passage opening up in front of him. It went down further a little way, and then seemed to begin stretching uphill under the ground beyond the wall of the basement in front of them.

"This is it, I know," said Sebastian, suddenly. "We never thought of looking on the ground, did we? We were so intent on searching the walls. We thought the entrance to the passage must be in the walls, but why should it not begin under the floor?"

Beattie started dancing for joy. "I'll never say I hate spiders again," she shrieked. "That spider and mouse who live down here have shown us the entrance to the passage." Then she added, "But can you see them down there? Are they crawling around?"

"Don't be silly," said Kevin, going down the steps after Sebastian. "This is so exciting, surely you are not going to let that put you off. Are you coming up the passage with us?"

"I sure am," said Beattie. "But as long as Sebastian goes first."

"Are you certain the passage is safe?" asked Tracy. She prided herself sometimes on being more sensible than Sebastian.

"Well, I'm shining my torch in front of me as I go," called back Sebastian. He had gone a little way up the passage and was waiting for the others. "I'm certainly not going to give up this adventure now. Now we've found the secret passage, I'm going up it."

Suddenly they all heard the bell for tea.

"Oh, no!" they all groaned in unison.

"We don't have to go," moaned Beattie. "Let's carry on up the passage and ignore it."

"No, we can't do that," said Kevin, irritably. "They will search for us and find us here. More than likely, they will stop us going up the passage. They will say it could be dangerous as it is so old and has been hidden for so long. This is our adventure. We'll come back after tea."

"Yes, I agree," said Sebastian. "This is our adventure and I want to go up the secret passage first. As I said before, this castle belonged to my ancestors."

"But do you think it might be dangerous?" suggested Tracy again. She suddenly felt sure that it was. It looked so dark and eerie inside.

"It's just a passage and the floor is quite solid," said Sebastian coming back along it. "We have good torches. We'll have tea quickly and then come back."

They all made their way back through the two basement rooms and up the steps out into the open air. They could hear Marjorie calling. She sounded irritated. A fierce wind was blowing their hair around, and rain was starting to lash down as they hurried round the outside wall of the castle to the kitchen door.

"I have been calling for you and ringing the bell for the last five minutes," Marjorie called out as she heard them approaching. "You know how Aunt Alice enjoys having tea in the afternoon at four o'clock and looks forward to us all joining her."

Suddenly she saw them come into the kitchen. She had been cooking at the Aga and she stopped dead. "What on earth have you been doing? You are absolutely filthy!" she shouted angrily. "Do you think you are going to sit at the tea table with Aunt Alice in that terrible state?"

"It's windy out there," said Beattie, pushing her tangled hair away from her face.

"Wind does not dirty your clothes and hair like that," said Marjorie furiously. "You will have to go and change your clothes. It's pouring with rain now. You are not going out again, today."

"We've got to go out again," whined Beattie. "We won't get wet in the rain at all – we were sheltering in the cellar."

"Shut up, you idiot," breathed Kevin.

Marjorie took the saucepan off the Aga and banged it down onto the table in front of her; then she turned angrily to look at them all. "Have you been down in that filthy cellar? I thought you would have more sense. I don't want you going down there again. I absolutely forbid you to go down into the cellar ever again. Go and get changed at once."

They all looked at each other in shock. This was disastrous! Tracy wondered why they had not noticed how dirty they were all getting. It was because of the excitement of finding the secret passage. Nothing else but that had seemed to matter to them.

Miserably the four of them left the kitchen. Kevin and Beattie took umbrellas from the umbrella stand in the hallway and made their way back to their cottage. Tracy and Sebastian went up to their bedrooms to take a shower and get changed into some clean clothes.

"I knew Beattie would give the game away and mess everything up," said Sebastian to Tracy as they went up the staircase.

Tracy didn't answer. Looking down at her clothes, she felt ashamed and embarrassed, but she realised that part of her was relieved that they were not going up the passage to the chamber of witchcraft that evening. She guessed though that she would be the only one of the party who felt that. The others must surely be mortified. They had been searching for the secret passage all day, and now they had found it and the entrance to it was wide open, they had been forbidden to go down into the cellar again.

★

When they were ready, they all came into the tea room and sat at the tea table. As usual it was piled up with good things to eat, but that did not cheer them up. Aunt Alice smiled at them benevolently.

"I am sure you were enjoying yourselves outside," she said, "but you must realise that the weather changes very suddenly here. It will probably rain all night now."

"Your father is going away to stay in town for a couple of days," said Marjorie, finally, to her son and daughter. "He's taking the car and will have to drive through this torrential rain tonight."

Tracy looked out of the window. "Yes, it's come on much stronger now," she said.

"I am sure it has really set in for the night," said Aunt Alice. "I think we are going to get a very bad storm. Are you afraid of thunder and lightning?"

"Of course not," replied Sebastian. "I rather like it. I like a dramatic storm, and you do have dramatic storms in the Highlands, don't you?"

"Yes, very often we do." said Marjorie. "Well, you're safe inside now, out of the rain, and we'll have an early dinner tonight since Wilfred will not be here."

She went to a cupboard and got out Monopoly and Cluedo boxed game sets. "Do you like playing games?" she asked. "We don't have a television here. We can all play games together."

Sebastian tried to suppress a groan, but Aunt Alice nodded in excitement. "Yes, we can all play a game together. I'd like that," she said. "If my eyes are not good enough, I am sure you young ones will help me."

"Yes," said Tracy politely. "But I'd rather not play Cluedo. It's a game about catching a murderer in a room in an old house, isn't it? We have to find out who the murderer is in the game."

Aunt Alice chuckled. "It's a detective game," she said. "Are you nervous here in this big, old spooky castle of mine? We are perfectly safe here. All right then, we'll play Monopoly."

For the next couple of hours they played Monopoly. Beattie had a sullen look on her face the whole time; Kevin looked as though he was desperately trying to hide his disappointment. Sebastian was lost in thought – *thinking about the treasure probably*, thought Tracy. She wondered if they were going to have to tell the adults about the passage now. How could they deliberately disobey Marjorie and go down into the cellar again?

"None of you are really concentrating on this game," said Marjorie after a while.

Sebastian raised his eyebrows. Aunt Alice looked as though she was dozing off too. It was obvious that only Marjorie was interested in the game.

"I'm going to serve the dinner now," Marjorie said suddenly, and got up to go out to the kitchen. "We'll finish this game another time."

Tracy went to help her set the table. They all sat down to eat – everybody except Wilfred who had left by car and braved it to go out in the storm. Dinner was followed by a supper of hot chocolate and biscuits.

At eight-thirty Marjorie collected up the mugs, and made a sign to Beattie and Kevin that it was time to go. It was still raining very hard, so they each took an umbrella from the stand in the hall again, and left by the back door.

"We'll all have an early night tonight," said Aunt Alice when they had gone. "When the storm hits us, as I am sure it will, I hope the thunder won't keep you awake."

Sure enough they all thought they heard a rumble of thunder in the distance.

"It's going to be a rough night. I hope you sleep well in spite of it," said Aunt Alice, again. "I shall take my hearing aids out, of course, so the storm won't bother me."

A feeling of dread and foreboding came over Tracy. The nights were bad enough as they were without thunder and lightning rolling around the house. Into her mind came a picture of the open entrance to the tunnel in the underground cellar leading up to the chamber of witchcraft. She shuddered. What horrors would that chamber hold, and what horrors did this night have in store for her?

Chapter Nine

THE GHOST IN THE PAINTING

Up the staircase they went again, stepping on each creaking stair.

Aunt Alice went into her room. Sebastian followed Tracy into her room; he seemed to have read her mind.

"Now," he said, as he closed Tracy's door behind him. "I have something to tell you, Tracy. We'll have no more imaginings tonight. There are no ghosts. Nobody was crying in the night."

Then he added, "If you heard somebody crying, I expect it was Beattie. You have seen how her mother is always getting annoyed with her."

"Poor Beattie. Is it because of us?" said Tracy.

"No, it's nothing to do with us at all – so forget it," said her brother fiercely.

"You don't like Beattie much, do you," said Tracy. "I know you blame her that Marjorie has forbidden us to go down into the cellar."

"Don't change the subject," said Sebastian. "I am talking about you terrifying yourself over ghostly things in the night that don't exist. Really, Tracy! It is always said that girls are more mature than boys, by two or three years, but that certainly isn't true in this place. I don't want to hear that you've had any ghostly experiences in the night, do you hear?"

Tracy began to sob. "I don't like it here anymore," she said. "I wish we had never come."

"Get into bed," said Sebastian impatiently. "You can keep the light on, but don't disturb me in the night." He went out of the room and slammed the door.

Tracy buried her face in her hands to stop herself crying. She kept the lights on, both of them, as she got changed for bed. The thunder was getting louder now, and Tracy could see flashes of lightning reflected through the glass in the window. There would be no moon tonight, surely. She went out to brush her teeth and came back. She sat on the bed. She wondered if she could stay awake all night, in case something happened. What could happen? She didn't know. Could that really have been Beattie crying last night? Surely she would not have heard her so far away in the cottage – unless, of course, Beattie was walking about in the night somewhere else. Could she have come up to the castle? Was Beattie so disturbed that she had left her bed? Tracy thought about it. But what about the other things: the things in the picture? Would she see them tonight? She sorely hoped not.

Slowly she looked up at the picture. It looked normal – its normal, bright sunny self that it was in the day. But it was always like this when she first went to bed, as though the picture didn't yet know it was night. It was only in the middle of the night that it changed: when she woke up in the middle of the night. Would it happen again? How could she go to sleep?

Tracy sat on the bed for what seemed like hours. She did not want to lie down. She could hear the torrential rain outside, and the thunder crashing all around the house. Every so often the lightning flashed again. Eventually exhaustion overtook her and she got into bed leaving both lights still on. She pulled the covers up around her. Tracy slept.

★

It was, again, in the middle of the night that Tracy awoke. The storm was still going strong. There was a gigantic flash of lightning across the room and then suddenly the lights went out – both of them. The storm had cut off the electricity supply. Horror of horrors! Tracy lay there in darkness, terrified.

She heard the sound of crying, again, quite

clearly. It was a girl crying, but it could not be Beattie. In fact, it sounded as if it was somebody in the same room as her. There was a soft glow in the room. Tracy knew what it was before she even looked up. She knew it was coming from the picture. The castle had found its night again.

Tracy felt for the bedside light switch and then remembered there was no light. She gave a little scream and then remembered she had a torch; she would get up and get it without looking at the picture. She would try not to look at the picture. The torch would give some light in the dark room, some comfort.

Torch in her hand she went back to bed. The torch was quite bright. Without meaning to she looked up at the picture as if something was willing her to. *Yes*, the castle was standing there in its night in an unearthly glow. She stared at the picture. Somehow she could not look away now: her eyes had become transfixed.

There was the cloud and the moon. There was no storm in the picture, just a moonlit night. And there was the girl leaning out of the window – the girl with a nightdress like Tracy's: pink with a frill around the neck. She could see her quite clearly – the girl was waving from the window. She was crying. The crying became louder. It was so pitiful. Then Tracy heard the girl call, "Help me."

The girl was calling for help. It looked to Tracy as though she was trapped in the castle in the painting and desperately wanted to get out. The crying continued and again she called for help, "Help me, please help me."

Tracy pulled the covers back and sat on the edge of the bed. She could not take her eyes away from the picture. She got up and felt her legs and feet moving towards it. There was something pulling Tracy closer and closer towards the painting, almost like a magnet. She could not resist. This was happening in spite of herself. She did not want to go towards the picture, she wanted to back away, but now she could do nothing about it. The picture itself was pulling her.

"Help me, help me," called the girl. Tracy's heart was filled with pity, and a desperate longing to help the girl.

"You're trapped inside the picture," whispered Tracy. "You're trapped. Somebody has to help you. Somebody has to help you get out."

The girl was crying more: so pitifully.

"I'll help you," said Tracy, "I'll help you."

She felt an acute empathy with the girl. The feeling became unbearable. She had to help the girl. She would have to go inside the painting to bring her out: to rescue her.

"I'm coming," she called. "I'm coming to bring

you out." The words spilled out of her mouth as though she could not stop them.

★

There seemed to be a mist enveloping her. She was getting lost in a mist.

Tracy heard a grotesque laugh. It was not the girl; it sounded like a man laughing. Tracy knew that she had heard it before: that evil sounding laugh. With a shudder she remembered the underground passage which they had left open, and which according to the map led up to the chamber of witchcraft.

Tracy could not stop looking at the girl in the picture. She had to get the girl out. She didn't know why she was feeling so passionately about it. It was as if somebody else was willing her to feel that.

The mist became thicker so that Tracy could not see anything at all. It was like a fog: thick and toxic. She suddenly felt so cold, as if she was outside in the cold, bitter night air. There seemed to be a gust of wind. She shuddered. What was happening?

The mist began to clear slowly. She could see a ray of light coming from above. Looking up, she saw it was the moon coming out from behind a cloud in the sky. The moon? How could it be? The sky was above her head. How could that be possible?

The mist had cleared completely now. Tracy

saw in front of her the castle – the castle!! She was outside, standing in front of the castle; not in her room anymore. How was this possible? She couldn't imagine how it was possible.

Tracy was on the drive, a little way from the front door. Around her were bushes and trees. She tried to switch on her torch, but it didn't work. She dropped it and ran up to the front door. She must get back into the castle again and up to her room, out of the cold. She didn't even have her dressing gown on.

As she reached the door she heard the crying again – much louder this time. It was coming from above her. Tracy looked up and saw the girl. She had shoulder-length brown hair which curled at her shoulders like Tracy's. Tracy didn't know which window she was leaning out of: there were so many rooms in the castle.

Tracy ran into the house. It was deathly silent and dark. She didn't know where the light switch was but she found her way to the main staircase. She ran up the stairs in the dark. There was no familiar creaking sound as there usually was. Tracy noticed this and it somehow unnerved her. There was a different feeling about the house entirely.

She ran along the dark corridor in the direction of her own bedroom. She knew instinctively where it was. She could hear the crying getting louder. The girl was in her own bedroom! Tracy was shocked. How could the girl be there, looking out of the window in her own bedroom? Was she real? She had looked very real to Tracy.

Tracy turned the door handle and opened the door wide. The crying stopped. It was pitch black in her room except that the moonlight seemed to be shining in through the window. Tracy knew that when she got used to the darkness she would be able to see better: to see shadows.

She felt for the light switch but there didn't seem to be one there. She closed the door behind her. Tracy stared into the room. She couldn't see the girl anymore. She moved closer to the window, but the girl was not there. There was no one there at all! She couldn't believe it. The room was cold, much colder than she had felt it before when she was inside. She looked around the room for her bed but it was not there. There was no bed in her room! There was no dressing table, no wardrobe, no shelves with books and ornaments – there was nothing. The room was bare and empty. The floor was of bare boards.

Tracy wondered if she had come into the wrong room by mistake. She made for the door, but horror of horrors – now even the door was not there anymore. There was no door, not even a wall, just a mist on that side of the room where Tracy had come in. She walked into the mist, but there was nothing. The mist went on and on, as if it went on forever. Tracy turned back into the room again where the moonlight was shining. At least the moon was still there; she could still see the window. She went towards it and looked out. There was no glass in the window.

Tracy screamed. She screamed and screamed. There was nobody there to hear her, she knew that. She was looking out of the high window, down onto the drive in the darkness of night. The moon was above her, peeping out from behind a cloud. Everything was silent and still: very, very still – deathly still.

Beyond the front driveway she could see that the gardens ended. There was something else there, something beyond it, as if she was looking out from another huge window beyond the first part of the garden. There were many shadows there. Tracy even thought that she could hear thunder in the distance, but it was not in her world, not in this garden.

Tracy knew now what had happened. She was in the picture, inside the castle in the painting. She was the girl in the picture. There was no one else. Somehow she had been enticed in here, she had been tricked, and now she was trapped. There was no way she could get out. The window was too high up the wall in the castle. It was a very, very long way down. And even if she could climb down, she would still be in the garden in that artificial moonlit night in the picture.

Tracy stood at the window, crying in her pink

frilled nightdress just as that girl had done, but she knew that the girl had been herself as she was now. Just for a moment, she remembered how, back at home, she had looked into the mirror and wished she could step into the world on the other side, into the picture in the mirror. Now, it was as though something like that had happened. She had stepped into the picture on her wall.

Tracy wondered if this was a nightmare, a terrible nightmare, but she could not wake up. She stood at the window for what seemed like hours crying, and then at last she slumped down on the bare wooden boards on the floor of the room. She fell asleep.

★

She slept for what seemed like a long time. Terrifying dreams filled her sleep; they didn't stop. When she woke up, the nightmare was still going on – she saw that her nightmare was real.

Somehow a light was shining into the room now. She didn't know from where it was coming. It seemed to be an artificial light coming from outside. She stood up and went to the window, but there was a mist over the window now. She could not see through it anymore. She could not see the garden outside.

She looked across the room towards the place where the door had been, where she had once entered. There was still no door there. There was only the same mist on the other side of the room. There was no way out – she was still trapped.

I will be trapped forever, she thought. *Who could ever know I was here, and if they did, how could they help me? But no one will know I am here. It is impossible. They will search and search in their world outside, but they will never find me. I will be gone forever.*

With that thought, she collapsed in anguish on the ground.

"I have been bewitched," she said to herself. "The eerie glow I saw around the painting must have been an evil magical witch's spell – dark, dark magic, so dark that it could draw me in, trap me here – here in this picture. I am in a prison."

For a moment Tracy thought she heard a voice: "So am I…"

It was a scornful, vengeful voice full of hate. Tracy stopped thinking. She had no energy to consider it anymore. She lay on the ground weeping. She fell asleep again, dreaming her nightmare. In her nightmare she saw a man; he was dressed in old-fashioned clothes, the kind she had seen in history books at school, worn by men about three or four hundred years ago. The man wore cream coloured knee-length breeches over what looked like white silk stockings. Frilled, lace shirt sleeves showed beneath the turned up cuffs of his green, velvet jacket, which he wore over a patterned gold-embroidered waistcoat. He wore his hair in a neat, shoulder-length curly, grey wig, and on his feet were black, gold-buckled shoes. His eyes were black and piercing. There was anger and hate in his eyes. The man in her nightmare came towards her.

In her dream, Tracy heard herself asking, "Who are you?"

"I am the Duke's youngest son, Sebastian," came the menacing reply. "I have the same name as your brother. And you are my prisoner. I have been trapped here for centuries and now you shall be here with me, a mere ghost in a picture, a ghost in the castle, a ghost of Creag Castle as I am."

"Nobody can be a ghost until they die," answered Tracy in her dream. She felt that her body had become light like a spirit.

"You shall be as dead now," said the ghost. "As you cannot get out, you must stay like this forever, here with me."

Tracy felt as though she was floating up and out of her body. In fact, she could see her body still lying on the ground beneath her. Her spirit body was rising up and the spirit of the ghost took her hand in his ghostly one.

"They will see you in the picture, but they will not be able to get you out." He laughed a horrible laugh.

Tracy was frozen with fear. The ghost turned

to go and then turned back to look at her. In that moment, Tracy thought she saw a glimmer of a different expression in his face, an expression of pain, sadness and longing; then it disappeared again.

"My father painted this picture," the ghost said. "I followed the spells in the witches' books to use the painting to put a curse on the castle out there, to burn it down, to destroy it, to destroy my brother – the favourite of my father. He left me nothing, nothing at all! The spell should have worked, but those witches' spells have a mind of their own. They are evil. They turn on the doer. The painting became bewitched instead and pulled me into its trickery, into itself. The power of the spell is so much that it can pull anybody who comes near it into itself. I have been here for a long time. Now it has managed to trap you, and I am jubilant. The dark magic has lasted all these years. It is still as powerful as the day it was unleashed. But the painting has been hidden away so long, for three or more centuries. Now it has been brought out from its hiding place and hangs on your wall. Now, I have my chance." He looked away and then added, "My chance – at last not to be alone here anymore in this hell. Now I have you."

Tracy was shaking all over. She could not even speak. She began to feel incredibly cold, and her spirit body seemed to slip back into her other body lying on the floor. The ghost of this Sebastian was disappearing into the mist on the other side of the room, where the door had been. Tracy was left alone to scream and cry in vain.

★

Meanwhile, Sebastian in his bedroom nearby was stirring. In his sleep he thought he heard a scream. In his sleep he dreamed a dream. Tracy had been captured by some evil spirits in the castle: evil spirits that lurked in the secret chamber at the end of the secret passage. The evil spirits took Tracy and used their magical spells to imprison her. He saw the painting on Tracy's wall; he saw the outside of the castle in the painting. He heard Tracy screaming again.

In his sleep, Sebastian got up and opened the door of his room. He went out along the passage in the dark and knocked on Tracy's door. There was no answer. He went in. All at once, he was mesmerised by the strange glow coming from the painting of the castle on Tracy's wall. Sebastian felt that he was sleep walking and could not wake up. He walked nearer to the painting. It was night in the picture. There were screams coming from it; there was a girl crying. He saw Tracy in the picture, leaning out of the window crying, "Help me." She was trapped in the picture.

Sebastian gasped and cried out. He could not wake up from his dream. It had to be a dream.

Chapter Ten

WHERE IS TRACY?

It was morning. Torrential rain was pouring down all around the castle: the real castle. Sebastian got out of bed and looked at his watch. It was twenty minutes past eight.

He washed and dressed and waited for Tracy to knock on his door as usual, but she didn't. The time went on: it was nearly nine o'clock. Where was Tracy? She was never usually late. He wanted to talk about the secret passage with her.

At last Sebastian went out to knock on Tracy's door. No answer. He knocked again and then he went in.

Tracy's bed was unmade, the covers were pulled back. She was not in the room. He went to look in the bathroom; she was not there.

"Where are you, Trace?" he called out. Still no answer. Sebastian felt annoyed. He wondered if she had gone downstairs without him. She must have done. He took himself down the stairs and entered the breakfast room. Marjorie was there at the Aga, as usual, and Aunt Alice was sitting in her armchair by the fire.

"Good morning, Sebastian," said Marjorie. "What a terrible morning it is with all this rain. We have no electricity at all in the castle. It is a good thing I have the Aga here for cooking. How did you sleep with that storm raging all night?" She looked around. "Where's Tracy?"

"I thought she was already down here," said Sebastian. "She's not in her bedroom."

"Is she in the bathroom, then?" asked Marjorie.

"No, she's not upstairs at all," said Sebastian.

"Well, she can't have gone out in all this rain, surely?" said Marjorie. "Have a look and see if she's sitting in the lounge. I haven't been in and made a fire in there yet."

Sebastian looked. He looked in all the other downstairs' rooms. "She's not anywhere," he said.

"Well, she has to be somewhere," said Marjorie.

"What's that?" asked Aunt Alice, who was just putting in her hearing aids.

"We've lost Tracy," said Marjorie. "She has not come down to breakfast and Sebastian can't find her anywhere. She's not in her room or in the bathroom, and she's not in any of these rooms downstairs."

Aunt Alice looked startled. "Good gracious,"

she said, "and the weather's so bad. Surely she can't have gone for a walk? Do you think she has gone over to your cottage to see Beattie and Kevin?"

Marjorie looked at the umbrella stand in the hall. "None of the umbrellas are gone," she said. "I wish she wouldn't do that, and before nine o'clock too, when I have the breakfast ready. I'll have to go and see if she's there."

Marjorie put on her raincoat and took the large umbrella out of the stand. "I'll be back soon," she said.

Ten minutes later she arrived back with Kevin and Beattie in tow.

"She's not there," said Marjorie. "Where on earth is she? Could she be in any of the rooms upstairs? She should not be walking around the house on her own going into the rooms."

They all went upstairs leaving Aunt Alice sitting in her armchair. Marjorie made them all keep together while they opened all the doors of the rooms, calling out to Tracy. They went up into the towers and up to the top floor. They looked everywhere and called out to Tracy, but there was no sign of her.

"Good gracious, she must have gone out in the rain. It is very, very silly of her and she'll be absolutely soaked. This is no weather to walk about in." said Marjorie.

They went back to the kitchen.

"We'll have breakfast," she said. "Perhaps she will come back soon. Perhaps she's sheltering somewhere in the gardens."

They ate breakfast in silence. Aunt Alice looked worried. "I hope you'll find her soon," she said.

After breakfast, Tracy did not appear. The rain had eased off a bit.

"We'll have to look for her in the gardens," said Marjorie. "You can look around the grounds together. You know the types of places where Tracy might have gone. I hope she hasn't fallen down on the muddy ground."

Beattie and Kevin put on their raincoats and took umbrellas from the stand. They put on their wellington boots that they had worn that morning when coming up from the cottage. Sebastian went to get his own boots and coat. They all made their way into the gardens. It was very wet and cold out there and there were many puddles. They searched everywhere around the grounds, but Tracy was not to be found.

"Do you think Tracy could have gone up the secret passage?" whispered Beattie.

"It's very unlikely," answered Sebastian. "She was scared enough of the idea of going up there even with the rest of us!"

They went to the cellar entrance and looked down the steps. They called out to Tracy.

"I'm sure she would not have gone down there," said Sebastian, "but where on earth is she? The only other place is the forest. It's quite worrying."

"Well, we have to search everywhere," said Beattie, "so we must go and tell Mum we need to search for Tracy in the cellar as we can't find her anywhere else. Good old Tracy. Now Mum will have to let us go down there."

They went back to tell Marjorie that they could not see Tracy anywhere, and that the only place they had not looked was the cellar.

Marjorie was making up the fire in the lounge for Aunt Alice. She turned to look at them. "Why on earth would she go down there again when I asked you not to?" said Marjorie crossly. "Would she have left something of hers down there yesterday and gone back for it? It's dark and the ground is uneven down there. She could have fallen down and sprained her ankle."

There was silence. Sebastian was feeling more and more anxious. He was sure that his sister would not have gone down into the cellar alone. "I can't imagine why she would run off anywhere, unless…" he said.

"Unless what?" asked Marjorie.

"She was frightened in her room last night," said Sebastian. "Not of the storm, but… our father told us this place might be haunted." He stopped speaking, then added, "and Tracy was getting a bit frightened at night. She started imagining she could hear noises in the night, and she was frightened of that painting on the wall."

"Of what painting?" put in Aunt Alice suddenly.

"That painting of the castle on her wall," said Sebastian.

"Good gracious. Why didn't she say so?" said Marjorie. "I thought she liked the picture."

"What picture is that?" asked Aunt Alice. "What picture did you put on her wall, Marjorie?"

"It was just a painting I found hidden away in one of the spare rooms," said Marjorie, "...such a lovely painting of the castle. I never thought she would be frightened of it."

"I'm going upstairs to look in her room in case she's left any clues as to where she's gone," said Sebastian, suddenly.

He went out of the kitchen and made his way to the great staircase and ran up it. Reaching Tracy's room he turned the door handle and went inside. He looked at her bed with the covers pulled back and then his eye caught the painting on the wall. He went over to it to have a look. This was the painting that Tracy had been so terrified of. He had not had any patience with her; he regretted that now. He remembered vaguely that he had seen the painting in his dream also.

He stared at it. It was a sunny picture, showing

the grounds and the stone walls and the towers of Creag Castle in all their glory. He looked at the battlements and at the painted wooden doors. He looked at the slit windows and at the dome-shaped windows, and then, suddenly, he saw her. He saw the face of a girl in pink, looking out of a window upstairs. The face appeared to be painted in: it was frozen in the picture, but he recognised it. It was the face of his sister, Tracy. Sebastian stared and stared. How could this be? How could anybody paint Tracy into the picture? He knew he was not dreaming now, and he knew without any doubt that the face had not been there in the picture yesterday. He had looked carefully at the windows, when Tracy had told him yesterday morning that she had seen a face there. He had told her she was imagining things.

Sebastian felt as though his heart had turned cold. He went downstairs and called out to Kevin and Beattie to come upstairs with him. They all entered Tracy's bedroom and Sebastian pointed to the painting.

Beattie gasped. She saw the face at the window at once and recognised it as Tracy's.

Suddenly they all heard a sound coming from the picture. It was like a very soft scream from someone who was just able to make herself heard. The face at the window in the picture moved: it was Tracy's. They heard her voice, "Help me." Then all was silent again; all was still again. The face of Tracy in the picture was again frozen into the picture.

They were all silent, staring. They were horrified.

"I had nightmares last night," said Sebastian, "about evil dark magic in the secret chamber." Then he paused. "We have opened up the passageway leading up to it, and we know from the map that it is also the chamber of witchcraft. Could it be that the magic has leaked out? We can see for ourselves what has happened to Tracy. This is dark, terrible magic. I never believed in magic at all before."

Then after a silence, he spoke again. "Whatever has happened, I have to get up that passage and into the chamber of witchcraft. This must have something to do with what is in that room. It is the only way for us to understand what has happened. If we are going to get an answer to this; if some dark, terrible magic has been put upon Tracy, I have to find out about it and how to reverse the magic and get her back."

Chapter Eleven

THE CHAMBER OF WITCHCRAFT

Sebastian raced downstairs with Kevin and Beattie at his heels, and went into the kitchen where Marjorie was cooking as usual. "We have got to look down in the cellar," said Sebastian. "There is nowhere else that we have not searched except the woods. You have to give us your permission."

"Very well," said Marjorie. "I hope she has not had an accident. Go and look down there, and take torches." She resumed her housework and Aunt Alice fell asleep by the fire.

The three of them raced outside and round to the back of the castle. "If you are going up the secret passage, then we are coming too," said Kevin. "Not just because we want to see where it goes, but because we want to help. We want to find Tracy."

"Absolutely," agreed Beattie. "We're all in this."

★

Down into the cellar basement they went, and through into the second room. At the end on the left-hand side was the hole in the ground with the stone steps going down, still uncovered. They had their torches with them still in their jacket pockets. All three of them went down the steps, one after the other, with Sebastian in the lead.

The passage was narrow and dark, and was beginning to rise uphill. The ground was paved with small loose stones and gravel which crunched under their feet. There appeared to be damp moss growing in cracks in the walls, which they could feel with their hands as they scrambled up the passage. At one point the ceiling became lower and they had to crawl on their hands and knees, but they kept going. There was only just enough air in the passage. Beattie was conscious of what felt like cobwebby threads hanging around her head from the ceiling, and she was sure she was not imagining spidery legs crawling across her ankles. She hated the passage but was determined not to turn back, to keep up with the others.

Sebastian kept going, determinedly. Finally he banged his knee on a hard surface in front of him. "We are here at the end of the passage, I think," he whispered.

They all shone their torches on what appeared to be a wooden wall in front of them. There didn't seem to be any handle on it, or any way to open it.

"This might be a door," said Sebastian. "Let's all push together and see if we can shift it."

Putting their torches down on the ground, but leaving them on, they all crouched down and, leaning against each other, gave a terrific push. To their surprise and delight, something gave way and the wooden door opened into another chamber. It was pitch-black. The three of them picked up their torches and shone them into the room.

They all gasped at the same time. Strewn on the floor were large, dusty, leather-bound books. Also an old metal cauldron lay in the corner on its side, filled with thick dust.

There were small ornaments and statues of figures lying around. When Sebastian looked more closely he saw that they were stone and metal images of grotesque-looking creatures, like witches and ogres and devils. Sebastian went and picked one up. It appeared to be a statue of an old hag, wearing a black cloak and hood with a horrible looking face. He picked up another ornament – it looked like a green goblin with an evil scowl, scrawny wings and long spindly arms with claw-like fingers and toes. Kevin picked up another one: it was a spiteful-looking figure with horns and a tail. In its protruding mouth there were pointed teeth and fangs. It wore an ugly grin, and looked as though it was about to pounce. There was a yellowish-coloured statue of a vampire-bat-like creature with huge wings and sharp teeth that looked as though blood was dripping from its mouth. Its talons were long and shaped like daggers. There were old broken candles of what looked like beeswax lying on the floor. Some old bones and a skull were lying in the corner of the room. Various old bottles lay about with some kind of coloured liquid inside. There was a heavy, old wooden table in the room. On it they could see carved illustrations of evil-looking snakes coiled up or about to attack, with their fangs hanging out. Everything was covered in thick dust.

"We are in the secret chamber next to the tower room," whispered Sebastian. He did not know why he was whispering, but it felt right to whisper in this place. "This is the chamber of witchcraft named on the map, and we can see why, with all these objects."

"This chamber has probably not been opened for about four hundred years," whispered back Kevin. "We must be the first ones to find this place and all these things."

"But there is supposed to be treasure in the secret chamber, isn't there?" said Beattie. "Is there any here?"

The chamber was small. They shone their torches all around the room, but there appeared to be nothing that looked remotely like treasure. Everything looked like implements of witchcraft – nothing else.

"Perhaps the treasure was stolen long ago," said Kevin.

"Or perhaps it never existed," said Sebastian. "Perhaps the people who owned the castle kept the passage hidden because witchcraft was against the law and they didn't want anyone to find the articles. Perhaps they were afraid of them too, so no one ever went up the passage or looked at them again."

He stopped speaking and stooped to wipe the dust off some of the huge books piled up on the floor. He read some of the titles of the books: *A Complete Book of Witchcraft*. Another book was entitled *Magic for the Night*, and yet another book was called *Invoking Spirits and Devils*. There was a book called *The Encyclopaedia of Magic*. There were some smaller books all containing witches' spells.

"I don't care about the treasure anymore anyway," said Sebastian. "I just want to get Tracy back. It could be because we have opened up this chamber that the evil magic has leaked out. There must be something here in this room that will help us – some information in these books of magic."

He tried to lift up the book entitled *A Complete Book of Witchcraft*. It was very heavy. He managed to heave it onto the table carved with evil-looking snakes. He opened a page of the book and dust clouds flew out and nearly choked him. The pages were yellow with age. There was an index at the beginning of the book inside the cover page, showing what the book contained. The first word of each sentence started with an ornamental letter, which appeared to be drawn and painted by hand. The contents of the book were listed in alphabetical order. It was like a dictionary of magic. Sebastian looked through the book. He looked under the letter 'C' and saw pages of spells for everything beginning with 'C'. There were spells for creating curses; there were spells involving cats and candles and carriages. Under the 'D's' were spells involving devils and dolls and diamonds. There were spells to make 'dreams come true' and to 'damage' something from a distance or to 'prevent damage'. Under the 'I's', incantations were listed; there were spells involving icicles and ink and irons; illnesses were listed that could be cured or caused. There were magical spells under all the letters of the alphabet to enhance your life and fulfill your desires – also to prevent others achieving their desires. There were love potions and lists of magical herbs and poisons and medicines.

"I just need to find something that can help me understand what has happened to Tracy," said Sebastian. Kevin and Beattie each heaved a heavy book onto the table and shone their torches on the pages as they turned them over.

"What exactly are we looking for?" asked Kevin in dismay.

"We have to find out what magical spell has been put on that painting," answered Sebastian. "It has become bewitched and Tracy is trapped there. We all saw her. If we can find out about the magic, perhaps we can also find out how to undo it."

There were no windows in the chamber and the dust was filthy. Beattie began coughing. At least new air was coming through the open passage from the cellar but the stuffiness of the enclosed space was making them feel unwell.

"Why would anybody put a spell on a painting?" asked Beattie.

In *The Complete Book of Witchcraft* Sebastian looked up the word 'painting' in the P's. There were all kinds of spells mentioned using painting as a method. One of them was to utter magic words while painting a picture of something you wanted to happen, or something you wanted to change or something you wanted to attract. There was a spell for making an object either disappear or grow bigger by painting it a certain colour. All the spells involved chanting magic words and performing certain rituals. There were so many spells for painting, but none seemed to be relevant.

"Look up the words 'trapped' or 'imprisoned'," suggested Kevin.

Sebastian looked up the words in the huge book. There was a spell for imprisoning somebody in a jar by making them much smaller.

"How absolutely horrible," said Beattie. "This is really frightening."

Sebastian looked up the word 'trapped'. There were spells for trapping ghosts. There was also a spell for creating an invisible net for catching hold of objects that seemed to be lost. He looked up the word 'bewitched'. Thousands of different spells were listed, but there seemed to be none which gave any insight into what had happened to Tracy.

"Perhaps we can find something in this other book," said Beattie, who was looking through the one entitled *Magic for the Night*. There were hundreds of ceremonies and rituals described and listed in the book – most of them highly unpleasant spells to make the lives of others a misery.

"No wonder this room was kept hidden," said Beattie. "There are so many pages of spells here and I don't know where to start looking."

Kevin was looking through the book entitled *Invoking Spirits and Devils*. It was full of pictures of evil-looking monsters, and spells for 'waking them up from sleep' as the book instructed.

"Do you think whoever was practising this dark magic actually did manage to 'wake up' any of these evil demons?" said Sebastian. Neither he nor Kevin could find anything in the book that would be remotely helpful in rescuing Tracy.

Kevin came over to look at the huge book in

front of Sebastian. "This is *The Complete Book of Witchcraft*," he said. "Surely we'll find something in this book."

"Yes, amid these thousands and thousands of spells," sighed Sebastian.

Then Kevin had an idea. "Look in the Contents section under the word 'picture'," he suggested.

Sebastian turned again to the spells listed in the 'P' section. He found 'picture'. Listed there were spells which used pictures of objects and places to bewitch the real thing. Sebastian and Kevin leaned over the book and began to read them.

"Look," said Kevin. "Listen to this: *A practitioner of magic may use a picture of an object or a place to put a spell on it which may be benevolent or malevolent. The larger the object to be bewitched, the more powerful is the magic needed to be created. When this spell is used for malevolent purposes to destroy a very large object or place, there is a risk that the very powerful dark magic created may produce an overwhelming heat that can engulf and kill the one creating the spell. Care must therefore be taken with the chanting and the ritual.*"

Sebastian read the next paragraph. "*If the malevolent magic becomes so powerful that it destroys the practitioner, killing him or her, then the spell is broken and the picture itself absorbs the magic instead of the object pictured. Then the picture, infused with strong evil magical powers, becomes like a magnet, and can draw into itself any soul that is near it, including the practitioner's, to trap it within itself. The powerful magic around the picture does not diminish with time.*

"That's it," gasped Sebastian. "Tracy has been drawn into that picture, literally."

Underneath the paragraph, the magic spell was written. There were instructions for a ritual which had to be done after midnight with a picture and a candle, and strange words to chant while the doer concentrates on his or her desired outcome.

Sebastian read the words of the spell. "But is there any antidote? Is there any way to reverse it?" he moaned.

There was the Roman numeral 'XX' next to the spell. At a sudden whim, Kevin turned the pages to the end of the book. There was a section entitled 'Extreme Magic'. Roman numerals again listed each paragraph. They found the 'XX' and both the boys strained to read what was there.

'XX: This powerful magical spell gone wrong cannot be reversed. Souls drawn into the bewitched picture must remain trapped unless another soul who feels genuine affection for the victim uses the same spell again benevolently, and enters the picture of his or her own free will to attempt a rescue. As the negative magic originally absorbed in the picture is so powerful and magnetic, this is fraught with danger and risk as the rescuer may himself easily be trapped in that realm along with the first victim.

'In order to introduce some element of protection while attempting such a rescue, the rescuer is advised while chanting the spell, to place beside a lit candle, a talisman of a heart-shaped object with the words 'love and freedom' on it or inside it. The rescuer must be single-pointed in his or her intent, having supreme sense of purpose, and distracted by nothing.'

Beattie came over to see what they were reading, and read it too. All three of them stood there in silence for a moment, seemingly shocked at what they had just read.

"Now we know," said Sebastian quietly. "I must create this spell tonight after midnight and attempt to rescue Tracy by entering the picture."

"What about us?" asked Beattie.

"I have to go alone," said Sebastian. "It's much too dangerous for all of us to go, and there's no need. Also, the book says Tracy has to be rescued by someone who feels some affection for her. I am her brother, so obviously it has to be me. I must rescue Tracy. Let's take this huge book with us out of here and take it up to Tracy's bedroom. I need the book to read the magic words."

The book was heavy, and Sebastian and Kevin carried it together down the secret passage, crawling on their knees again in the low-ceilinged part of the cellar. Beattie went first, in front of them both. She was so eager to get out of there. They all were. At last they climbed the steps and came up into the cellar room. Sebastian took off his rain coat and covered the book, as they walked out into the open air through the cellar door. It had just about stopped raining. What a relief it was to get out into the fresh air. They went round to the side of the castle and entered through a back door. Quietly they all climbed the small staircase at the back of the house. They did not want to be seen by Marjorie or Aunt Alice just yet. Once in Tracy's bedroom, Sebastian opened the large book on the floor and read the instructions for the spell again.

"We need a candle to be placed on the floor in front of the painting," he said.

"I know where some candles are kept in a cupboard in the castle." said Beattie.

"What are we going to do for a heart-shaped talisman?" asked Kevin.

"We can use my silver locket on a chain, can't we?" suggested Beattie. She unfastened it from around her neck and showed it to them. "Look, it's heart shaped and it opens up. We could put a slip of paper inside with the words 'love and freedom' written on it."

"That's a brilliant idea," said Sebastian. "Thank you Beattie. I would never have thought of anything like that." Beattie glowed with pleasure at Sebastian's praise.

They hid the large book of witchcraft under Tracy's bed.

"I need to fetch the candle and matches to light it with," said Sebastian, "and then we just have to wait for the night to come. Are you willing to come here at midnight and sit with me while I perform the ritual?"

"Of course we are," said Kevin and Beattie together.

"We'll sit here until you come back with Tracy, even if it takes all night," said Beattie.

"I hope it won't," answered Sebastian. Then suddenly he looked at the clock on Tracy's bedside table and gasped. "It's five minutes to one. We have to get down to lunch at one o'clock. Quickly, let's brush the dust off our clothes. Whatever are we going to say to your mother and Aunt Alice? They are going to expect us to have found Tracy."

"We'll just have to tell them we haven't," answered Kevin. "There is no way we can tell them what has really happened."

They all went over to look at the painting. Tracy's face was staring out of her window on the first floor of the castle in the picture, but it looked absolutely frozen there, just a painted face, without any movement at all. Anybody who had not seen the face move or heard its gentle scream earlier, would never believe that it was really Tracy. They would believe it just to be a face in the painting of a girl who resembled Tracy. Nobody would ever be able to believe what had really happened.

Quietly they left Tracy's room and made their way down to the lunch room. It was not going to be a happy meal.

Chapter Twelve

THE MAGIC RITUAL

Marjorie was just taking the hot food into the lunch room when Sebastian, Kevin and Beattie arrived.

"There you are," she said anxiously. "Have you found Tracy?"

"No, I'm afraid we haven't," muttered Kevin.

"Wha-at!" shrieked Marjorie. "You still haven't found her? How could you not have? Whatever has happened to her?"

The three of them stood there in silence.

"She must be lost in the woods!" Marjorie's voice rose into a shrill, fearful wail.

Aunt Alice looked up startled from her armchair by the fire. "What has happened?" she asked.

Marjorie burst into tears. "Tracy is missing," she cried. "I am responsible for her. I spoke to her mother over the phone. I assured her I would be taking care of her children here."

Aunt Alice got up slowly from her chair to go and sit at the table.

"That's a worry," she said. "But perhaps she has just gone for a very long walk. It's not raining any more is it?"

"She would easily get lost in the woods if she has gone walking there," cried Marjorie desperately. "It will be so muddy in the forest, and if she fell down or slipped into a marshy pond she might not be able to get out again."

"We'll go into the woods this afternoon," said Kevin, trying to comfort his mother.

"I'll come with you," said Marjorie quietly. "You must not go alone. We must tie ribbons onto the trees as we usually do so that we can find our way back safely."

They all sat down to eat in silence. Nobody knew what to say. They knew that Marjorie would want to go on searching, and they knew that Tracy would not be found.

"We can't even call anybody to help in the search," cried Marjorie, "because the telephone lines came down in the storm last night. We have no way to phone. We don't even have a car to go anywhere, because Wilfred has taken it and won't be home until tomorrow night."

After lunch they all went to get their raincoats in case the rain started again. It was very damp outside and rainwater was dripping from the trees and from the roof everywhere. Leaving Aunt Alice asleep in her armchair by a roaring fire, they all went off in the direction of the woods. First they went to the old summerhouse where Beattie and Kevin kept a large tin of red ribbons to tie to the trees when they went orienteering in the forest.

They walked in the woods for about three hours. It was very muddy. They followed all kinds of paths, tying the ribbons to the trees as they went to make sure they did not get lost. The ground was marshy in places, and especially when they walked around a small flooded pond.

"There is nothing we could do this afternoon anyway," whispered Kevin to Sebastian. "We have to pretend to keep looking, for Mum's sake, otherwise she will get hysterical."

At four-thirty they made their way back to the castle as Marjorie knew that Aunt Alice would be waiting for her tea. She rushed into the kitchen in a frantic state.

"If only Wilfred was here," she cried. "He would know what to do. He would call out a search party. There is nothing we can do until he comes home tomorrow night."

Marjorie made tea and toast for Aunt Alice. Beattie brought in the crockery and the cutlery, and Kevin brought in some more logs for the fire. It was no longer raining; however, it was cold in the evening. As there was no electricity, Marjorie took a paraffin lamp out of the cupboard ready for their use later. Everything she did in silence, but her eyes were red and sad-looking.

She cooked the dinner for them all and when it was ready she served it in the large dining room, first laying the table. She set out the plates.

They sat silently on armchairs in the lounge after dinner. Aunt Alice fell asleep again. There were no board games that evening.

The grandfather clock in the hall chimed eight times. It was only eight o'clock. Sebastian went upstairs to get his laptop and a computer game to play to try to stop himself worrying too much. He thought he might faint with apprehension and misery thinking about the task ahead. He invited Kevin and Beattie to play a computer game with him, but try as they did, they could not even begin to play the game. They could not concentrate on it for even one second. Their minds wandered continually. Eventually they gave up.

Marjorie finished the washing up and then called to Kevin and Beattie to follow her back to the cottage for the night. As they went out, Sebastian gestured to Kevin and he made a sign back. It was an affirmation that he and Beattie would find a way to come back at midnight. They would not leave Sebastian to face this frightening ordeal alone.

When they had gone, Aunt Alice went around the house with the paraffin lamp, locking up, bolting the doors as usual, even though she always said they were completely safe in the castle. However, she left the kitchen door unlocked. "Just in case Tracy comes back tonight," she said. "I do hope she has found somewhere out there where she can shelter until we find her. There are a couple of little stone chalets used years ago by hikers, a few miles into the forest. Tomorrow we will call out a search party as soon as Wilfred returns."

As they went up the stairs, she turned to Sebastian. "Try to get some sleep, my dear," she said. "Worrying will not bring Tracy back tonight. I will pray for her safe return tomorrow. We can only hope for the best."

Sebastian remained silent. He was feeling increasingly upset and worried. He was desperate to rescue Tracy. He knew he still had three hours to wait until midnight. If only this night was over and they could all be together again safe. If only it would be successful – there was no knowing if it would be; even the book of witchcraft said that the operation was a huge risk.

★

After Aunt Alice closed the door of her bedroom, Sebastian waited for half an hour to make sure she was asleep with the light off. He then crept downstairs to look for a candle in a cupboard in the dining room. Beattie had pointed out the cupboard to him earlier that day. Finding the candles in a box, he took out a large, thick, white one and then searched for a box of matches. He found a box in the kitchen near the Aga and then crept back up the staircase again, and tiptoed along the corridor so as not to awaken Aunt Alice. If she had not left the kitchen door unlocked, Sebastian would have unlocked it. Every morning Kevin and Beattie entered the castle through that door after breakfast, so he guessed they would come in that way tonight.

Very quietly, Sebastian opened the door into Tracy's bedroom. The hours passed slowly for him. He sat for a long time on her bed, gazing at the painting on the wall. Tracy's face still appeared to be frozen into the picture without moving, without any sound. Somehow she had found the strength to defy the magic and cry out when Beattie and Kevin had come into the bedroom with him that morning. That was proof that she was still alive. That gave him hope. Perhaps that night they would see her moving again at the window in the painting. The benevolent spell had to work: Sebastian would ask the magic to bring Tracy out of the picture. He would enter the painting by means of the magic spell and rescue her, if only he could.

At twenty minutes to twelve, some distance away in the Jefferson's cottage, Kevin knocked on Beattie's bedroom door. Beattie got out of bed and got dressed quickly. She took her silver heart-shaped locket out of her jewellery box where she had placed it when she went to bed. She looked at it and wondered if it would matter that it had engravings of a rose flower on the front, and an angel's head and shoulders with wings at the back of it. The magic spell had not said anything about that. She found a piece of white paper and a pair of scissors and cut out the shape of a small heart. In felt-tipped pen, she wrote the words 'love and freedom' on it. She opened the locket and slipped the paper heart inside. It fitted exactly.

Placing the locket around her neck, Beattie fastened it with the silver chain. She and Kevin passed silently along the corridor. Kevin had heard Marjorie sobbing in her room when he had first got up, but now there was silence coming from there – so it appeared that she had at last gone to sleep.

Greatly relieved, the two of them went to the cupboard and got their torches. In the garden it would be pitch-black and they would have to find their way up to the castle. It was not far, but they wanted to get there before midnight to help Sebastian prepare for the magic spell.

They made their way to the kitchen door of the castle and finding it open, they quietly crept up the corridor to the smaller staircase at the other end of the house, to climb to the first floor. This felt safer as they knew they would not have to pass Aunt Alice's room to get to Tracy's room. When they arrived at Tracy's door, Kevin knocked gently. He carefully opened it and he and Beattie crept in.

★

Sebastian turned to his friends gratefully as they entered, and gestured to them to sit on the cushions he had set out on the floor. He had already set up the candle beneath the painting on the wall. Beattie unfastened the heart-shaped locket around her neck and put it down beside the candle.

It was five minutes to twelve. Sebastian got up from the bed where he had been sitting and lit the candle with a match. He turned off the main light, and then sat on a cushion with his friends in front of the painting on the wall. He had *The Complete Book of Witchcraft* open at the page with the magic words of the spell that he was going to read. Kevin and Beattie sat with their legs crossed in silence next to him. They were all waiting for the large grandfather clock in the hall to chime twelve times.

Sebastian closed his eyes, waiting for the chimes. At last they came. At the twelfth chime, he put his hands on his heart as the book instructed. He opened his eyes and began to chant the words of the spell, over and over again.

An eerie glow was now emanating from the painting. The picture was beginning to change. Beattie and Kevin stared in amazement as they watched the sky in the painting become dark. A moon was peeping out from behind a cloud where the sun had been before. Suddenly there was a sinister, gloomy aura of night around the castle in the picture. The face of Tracy looking out of the first-floor window, which had been frozen there before, started to move. Sebastian gasped, half in delight and half in terror. There was a soft sound as if someone was calling in the distance, "Help me, help me." It was Tracy.

"I'm coming," said Sebastian. He stood up.

All at once there appeared a boy's face in the window of another room in the picture of the castle. It was also calling out for help.

"Wait," gasped Beattie. "Something very weird is happening."

"Yes, hold on," whispered Kevin anxiously, "That boy looks exactly like you, Sebastian. What's going on?"

"It's not me," Sebastian said. "How can it be? It must be somebody else. Perhaps I will have to rescue him too."

"I think it might be some kind of trick to distract you from Tracy," warned Kevin desperately. "Remember you have to rescue Tracy. The book says you have to be single-minded. Go in there and quickly bring her out. Don't pay attention to anything else."

Sebastian felt an overwhelming desire to rescue the boy, too. He seemed to be pleading with Sebastian with his eyes. How could he go in there and not help the boy as well? How could he not help them both?

A mist was forming in the bedroom. Sebastian got up and walked up close to the painting. The mist was engulfing him. He could not see anything anymore. It was becoming thicker and thicker, and he was beginning to feel very cold. Suddenly he thought he heard an unpleasant laugh. It was the sound of someone full of glee. Sebastian shuddered.

The mist was clearing. Sebastian was shivering. He was out in the open air – in the night air without a jacket! He was standing in front of the castle. For a moment he wondered what had gone wrong. What was he doing outside? He would have to go back into the castle and climb the stairs again, and start all over again. He looked up at the moon in the sky peeping out from behind a cloud. Then he heard crying: Tracy's crying. He knew it was Tracy. He looked upwards again and saw Tracy leaning out of the window. She was life-size now. He realised where he was – he was in the painting, outside the castle. Terror filled his whole being. There was somebody else calling for help in another window. It was the boy he had seen before. Sebastian ran towards the door of the castle shouting, "I'm coming."

It seemed that Tracy had heard him. She cried out to him and then she stopped and screamed. She was shouting something, but Sebastian did not wait to hear what it was. He ran into the castle. It was pitch-black, but he found his way to the staircase. He climbed the stairs and stopped where he knew that the stairs gave way to the first floor – where he knew their bedrooms were.

Now he could see a glow in the corridor that seemed to be coming from under the doors in the rooms. The same glow was coming from under his own bedroom door. He could hear the boy calling from that room: his own room! That boy was in his room in the picture. Sebastian felt desperate to get him out: to rescue him first. Perhaps it would be a good idea. He could go there, rescue the boy, and perhaps the boy would help him. Together they could bring Tracy out.

He moved towards the door of his room. It even seemed to be a little ajar now as if it was inviting him to enter.

Sebastian took the door handle in his hand and flung the door open. He thought he could see the boy at the window. He let go of the door handle and ran in towards the window. To his utter surprise there was no one there. The room was completely empty. He looked back and saw that the other side of the room was engulfed in a thick mist. The door and even the wall had disappeared. There was no furniture at all in the room. Desperately he tried to run back, but there was no way of escape. He tried and tried to get through the mist, but there was nothing there anymore – the mist seemed to go on forever. He was trapped in his own room in the picture.

A gleeful laugh rang out. It was the same ugly laugh he had heard before. A voice seemed to shriek triumphantly in his ear, "Now I have two of you as my prisoners."

Sebastian looked around to see the ghost of a man dressed in seventeenth-century clothes with a grey wig. His eyes were black and full of anger.

"I am the Duke's youngest son and you are my prize prisoner," said the ghost, "because you are also called Sebastian. You are my namesake, and you are also an heir to this castle, but now you will never own the castle as I was not allowed to own it. I am dead, and I haunt the real castle as well as this picture, but you will never be able to leave the picture now – you will stay in the painting forever and you will never be able to return to your world."

Chapter Thirteen

THE DEMONS IN THE PAINTING

The ghost disappeared into the mist as suddenly as he had appeared. Sebastian was numb with fear and shock. He went back to the window and stared out. He saw the garden in the painting in front of him, heavy like indigo and purple strokes of a paint brush in the artificial darkness. The moon above was like a white disc drawn with crayon against a paint-sprayed cloud. This world was frozen and two dimensional, unlike the world outside. He was to be a frozen figure in a canvas, like Tracy.

He had no chance of rescuing her or rescuing himself now. Sebastian closed his eyes and prayed that this was a nightmare from which he would soon wake up. He opened them again and leaned out of the window as he had seen Tracy do from her window. He could not see Tracy, and he could not see Kevin and Beattie out there. There seemed to be large shadows of a kind that he could not identify in the distance. Was it them? Could it be Kevin and Beattie? In a last burst of energy, he called out: "Help me, help me," just as Tracy had done.

★

Meanwhile, Kevin and Beattie had been watching and waiting. They had seen the mist form around Sebastian while he was chanting and they had seen him disappear into thin air. They had seen the boy at the window calling for help. The figure of Tracy was still crying in the other window.

Silently Kevin and Beattie sat there waiting. They waited in the desperate hope that Sebastian and Tracy would miraculously return. More than an hour passed, but nothing seemed to be changing in the picture. Tracy was still there at the window, trapped, and so was the face that looked like Sebastian's.

Suddenly Kevin got up wearily. "I know what's happened," he said. "Sebastian has also become trapped there. The evil spell has taken him. We have lost them both."

Beattie started to cry. "It can't be true," she said. "Sebastian is such an intelligent boy. How could that happen to him? How could the magic not work?"

"It has worked," groaned Kevin, "but the evil magic engulfing the picture is so powerful, as the book said, that Sebastian was not able to defend himself against it. He has been drawn into the painting like Tracy, and it looks as if he didn't even get a chance to meet her there at all. He is trapped in his own room in the painting. That is the window of his own room in the real castle."

"But what can we do?" shrieked Beattie.

"I am going to chant the spell and enter the picture to try to rescue them both," said Kevin determinedly. "That is the only thing we can do. I will be single-minded and will not allow myself to be distracted by anything. I will simply go in there with supreme sense of purpose, just as the book says."

"Oh, no, don't do that," begged Beattie in tears. "You can't leave me here alone. If you go in there, you will also get stuck in the picture, I know it. It is so terrible. Please don't do it. I can't bear it."

"No, I must do it," insisted Kevin. "We have the magic spell in front of us and this may be the only chance. I am certain I can get them out. The book says it is possible. We have the heart talisman here to protect us. I just need to be strong and have absolute trust in the spell."

Kevin looked into the huge book of witchcraft and began chanting the spell with his hands on his heart. He concentrated on the task ahead. In the darkened castle in the picture, a face appeared in an upstairs room. It was the face of Kevin.

Beattie screamed. She knew that if Aunt Alice had not taken out her hearing aids she would have heard her.

Kevin stopped chanting. Both he and Beattie leaned forward to look. The face of Kevin was leaning out of a window high up on the fourth floor next to the tower on the left side of the picture. They both knew there was no window there in the real castle.

"That is the tower with the secret chamber – the witches' room," cried Beattie in horror, "Look! Do you think that face which is pretending to be you is in the chamber of witchcraft?"

Kevin could not speak for shock. "I know it's a trick," he said. "Luckily I know it's a trick because we saw what happened with Sebastian. Sebastian was duped into thinking there was someone else who was crying for help. I won't be duped. I don't have a bedroom in this castle, so I will not be so easily persuaded to enter a room that isn't mine. I will not go anywhere near that fourth floor room no matter how much that figure calls for help."

Beattie hugged Kevin. "Please don't go," she said. "It's still a terrible risk. The dark magic all comes from that chamber, so the energy that is coming from there is bound to be powerful. How will you be able to resist its pull? It has a magnetic pull."

"I know that," said Kevin. "But I have no choice. I am going in to try and bring them out."

"Then I am coming with you," screeched Beattie.

"Oh, no you are not," shouted Kevin, and he pushed Beattie away from him. She was clinging to his waist. "Two of us can't go together. The book says nothing about two people going at the same time, and I don't want the trouble of having to rescue you as well!"

"The book says that the rescuer has to be someone who feels some affection for the victim," spluttered Beattie through her tears.

"Well, they are our friends," said Kevin, "so perhaps that is enough."

With that, he sat down on the ground cross-legged in front of the candle that was still burning, and began to chant again.

Beattie covered her face with her hands. She did not want to look. Kevin stood up, walked towards the painting and also disappeared into a mist. He was gone. Beattie opened her eyes and saw that he was gone. Upstairs in the fourth-floor chamber next to the tower in the painting, the face of Kevin looked down, calling for help. The face of Sebastian looked anxiously out of the window of Sebastian's bedroom in the picture. The face of Tracy was still there, as it had been yesterday when Beattie had first set eyes on her friend trapped in the painting.

Beattie was in shock. Surely this was a nightmare! She stared and stared at the painting. Was it really them, or was it still a trick to entice more people in, to trap them in that terrible prison? But if it was not them, then where were they? *They must be trapped in the picture, it must be true*, thought Beattie.

She was determined to believe that it was not Kevin, after all. He would come out and perhaps he would be able to rescue Tracy and Sebastian. He must rescue them. She just had to wait – there was nothing else to do.

★

Meanwhile, Kevin had entered the mist and found himself outside the castle in the picture as Tracy and Sebastian had done. He also was totally confused by it. He stood outside the castle in the night and looked up at the moon coming out from behind a cloud. It never actually came out completely from behind the cloud. It was frozen in that position. Above Kevin, were the windows of the castle. He could see the faces at the windows and he could see that they were Sebastian and Tracy, life-size now.

Tracy seemed to see him, and called out. He could hear Sebastian also calling out, but Sebastian was shouting, "Go back, go back, Kevin."

The figure leaning out of the window in the chamber next to the tower on the fourth floor, was shouting to him for help.

Kevin yelled back to the boy. "I'm not coming to you. You can scream forever in that place. You'll not entice me in there. I'm not a fool. I know you are some malevolent being in disguise."

"You will stay in this room forever," called the boy in a sneering voice. "You will not be able to resist coming here to me. I am your future. I am you, here in this room." Then he added mockingly, "You will have to come and rescue me first or you will never get out."

"That is your trick to get me there," shouted Kevin. "You have duped both Sebastian and Tracy, but you will not dupe me. I will rescue them and I will never come near you."

Kevin ran into the castle and started to run up the hollow sounding staircase in the ghost house. He wanted to go to Tracy's room first. There was suddenly a horrible laugh on the stairs in front of him and there stood the ghost of the man dressed in late seventeenth-century clothes, barring his way.

"Did you think you could rescue my prisoners?" said the ghost, sneering. "I have waited for centuries for them, for their company here. Do you think I am going to let them go so easily?"

"Let me pass," shouted Kevin. "I will rescue them. I will take them out of this prison."

All at once there was a wailing, growling, snarling noise coming from another part of the castle, from a higher floor.

The ghost laughed his horrible laugh again. "You have awoken the devils upstairs in the secret chamber," he shouted. "What a pity for you; now you will have to answer to them, just as I have had to, all these years."

The next moment, Kevin became aware, amid the noise, of a green ogre-like monster with one eye in the middle of its forehead running down the stairs, two steps at a time, to attack him. It was bigger than him and it charged at him and knocked him to the bottom of the staircase. Kevin yelled out. The next moment the ogre grabbed Kevin roughly and lifted him high into the air above its muscular arms. It carried him along the corridor to the tower steps and raced with him up to the fourth floor. There the ogre crashed through a gap in the wall of the tower, exposing the secret chamber on the other side. He threw Kevin onto the ground.

The room was packed with life-sized grotesque, monstrous-looking creatures of all shapes and colours – the ugliest looking beings Kevin had ever set eyes upon. They looked as though they were stirring and beginning to move after sleep. Some were already standing up and roaring, and some were beginning to flap their scaled wings and swing their armour-like tails. Others were sharpening their claws and talons and gnashing their razor-like teeth. Kevin recognized them as the ornaments and statues of demons, devils and goblin-like creatures that he had seen in the secret chamber in the real castle. There they had been mere ornaments and statues – here they were huge – all bigger than Kevin himself. These creatures were alive in this chamber, in the ghostly world of the painting.

A hideous old hag in a black cloak stood up and waved her finger at Kevin. She had long, sharp, pointed fingernails that shone. She cackled a witch's laugh. Kevin remembered that Sebastian had picked up the statue of this witch in the secret chamber of the real castle.

"We will have you in here with us," cackled the witch, nastily. She opened her mouth and revealed two broken pearly teeth.

An orange demon with ruby red eyes, long spindly arms and a huge head with fangs sticking out of its protruding mouth, dragged Kevin up from the ground. A green devil with a yellow forked tail held a long, sharp pin in his claw-like fingers. He stuck it into Kevin's neck, so that Kevin cried out in pain. No blood escaped from his body. Kevin noticed that his body had become transparent and jelly-like: a spirit body. He reflected that probably nobody could die in this ghostly castle – he could suffer pain and unhappiness and torment, but would remain here, unchanged, forever in this prison.

A winged, red devil roughly dragged Kevin

towards the window and forced him to lean out. Other demons pressed against him so that he could hardly breathe. They pierced him with their horns and talons, and bit him with their sharp teeth. They clubbed him with their armoured tails and clawed at him with their sharp nails.

Kevin called from the window. There was nothing else he could do. He guessed that he would never be let out of this room again. The devils would imprison him and torture him forever. The malevolent magic in this room was too powerful for him. He had not bargained for that. There was nothing he could do now. He wondered if the demons, now awake, would also be able to go and torture Tracy and Sebastian in their prison cells, on the first floor of the castle in the painting.

Chapter Fourteen

THE SILVER HEART

In Tracy's bedroom in the real castle, Beattie waited and waited. Kevin must come out soon surely. It could not be him looking out of the window of that terrible room next to the tower on the fourth floor. Beattie would not allow herself even to imagine it for a second. *Kevin must be busy finding a way to rescue our friends*, she thought. He would not be duped into going into that chamber. He was not so foolish.

For three and a half hours Beattie waited. She began to feel weak with dread and despair. Surely this terrible thing had not happened to all three of them. It couldn't have. Was she really alone now?

The candle had nearly burned down: soon it would be going out; soon it would be all over; it would be too late. She could even see in the corner of her eye that the dawn outside in her own sky was beginning to show its first pale light – soon it would be morning.

Beattie thrust out her hands and snatched up the

silver locket. She clasped it in her palms and fastened it with the chain around her neck. She grabbed at the book of witchcraft and began to chant. She chanted with all her strength. The mist appeared in front of the castle and Beattie stood up and walked into it. As she did so, a girl's face appeared at another window higher up in the tower. Beattie did not even notice it.

She was outside the castle now. It was so cold. She shivered and shivered. She could see Tracy and Sebastian and Kevin all leaning out of the windows, life-size above her. She did not even stop to think where she was. They were all shouting to her, "Go back, go back."

Beattie took no notice. She ran through the huge, painted wooden door of the castle at the front and along the empty, ghostly corridor to the enormous staircase. All at once it felt as though a great whirlwind hit her and tried to lift her up. A whole army of hideous-looking monsters were tearing down the staircase towards her, growling and snarling and roaring as they did so. The devils from the secret chamber in this ghostly world were all awake now. They flew at her and threw themselves upon her. Beattie screamed for all she was worth. She collapsed on the floor. The demons were piercing and biting and squeezing her. One of them changed itself into a huge snake that wrapped itself around her; another one was clawing at her eyes. All at once, an enormous vampire-bat-like devil bared its teeth and took a bite at her neck.

Suddenly, the silver chain of her heart-shaped locket snapped in two, and the silver heart flew into the air.

It happened so quickly. The engraving of the rose flower on the locket began to come to life, and the rose petals started falling and floating all around and landing everywhere on the creatures in the hallway. As they fell around and landed on the grotesque creatures, the beautiful petals touched them and burned their skin. The demons screamed out in pain. As the locket also fell, the small piece of paper with the words 'love and freedom' fell out onto the ground. The silver heart hit the ground and rolled on the floor and came to life itself and started beating. Suddenly, the engraving of the angel on the back of the locket also came to life. A tall, beautiful being surrounded by silver light and fragile silver wings rose up tall, and stood in front of them all. Her light filled the whole hallway where they were; the light seemed to fill the whole castle.

The devilish creatures all around were screaming and cowering in terror at the sight of the angel towering above them. They started shrinking and melting in her glorious light, becoming smaller and smaller. Finally, they rolled about on the floor, becoming mere statues and ornaments like the ones in the chamber in the real castle. They lay lifeless on the ground, useless and harmless.

All at once, there was another scream. The ghost of the first Sebastian, the Duke's son, suddenly appeared and collapsed on the floor in front of the angel. He stared up at her in utter awe and terror as he lay at her feet.

"Forgive me, forgive me," he cried. "Have mercy on my soul. Take me out of this terrible, dark place, this hell, this prison. I have been here alone for so long. I can't bear it here alone any longer."

The angel stood there in all her glory.

At that moment, Tracy and Sebastian and Kevin came running down the main staircase in utter joy. They had suddenly found that the mist on the walls of their prisons had lifted and the open doorway in each of their cells had appeared again, setting them free. Beattie gasped at the sight of her brother and her friends. They all gazed up at the angel, and stared down at the ghost of the first Sebastian in amazement.

"Has he also been trapped here in this place, like I was?" asked Tracy. "In this terrible place for so long, in such misery and such terror as I have known? Look at his old-fashioned clothes! Oh, then please help him to come out also."

Her brother Sebastian stared at her.

"I am sorry, I am so, so sorry…" cried the ghost, still lying at the feet of the angel.

The angel shone all the more brightly. "My name is Love," she said. "And my second name is Freedom. Love always gives freedom."

She turned to the ghost, "You are free," she said. She touched his forehead. The ghost of Sebastian cried like a small child at the angel's feet.

"You are out of your prison," the angel said to him. "You have suffered enough in this life and death, and you created this hell for yourself. The door out of here has always been there, and it has always been open for you, but you just couldn't see it. You just need eyes of love. You need to forgive what seemed unfair to you in your life. Now you can go out into the garden of Heaven into a higher dimension, where you shall find the happiness that you never knew in your life here on this earth."

Sebastian and Tracy stared at her. They also could both see that the great door of the castle in front of them was wide open. The ghost of Sebastian, the first Duke's son, ran out of the great door and into the garden in utter joy.

Beattie was looking on the ground for her silver locket. The angel stooped and picked it up. The heart became a silver locket again in the hand of the angel. She smiled at Beattie and gave her the locket, and then she gestured for the children to follow her out of the castle. The angel went ahead of them all. Her light seemed to be as bright as a thousand suns that would not burn them. They all gazed at her: she had a beauty and grace not of this world.

"I would like to look at her for the rest of my life," said Tracy in wonder, "and never take my eyes away."

The angel led them out of the castle. She led them along the first part of the drive until they came to a thick mist.

"This mist does not really exist," said the angel. "You just have to know that the light is always with you and you are never alone. Then you need never be afraid of anything anymore. Then there is no mist anywhere and you are free and you can see that the dimension of Heaven is always around you – everywhere. You only have to open your eyes and see it. Eyes of love can see it. You will see that there are angels everywhere in the light, and they will come and help you if you call on them."

Tracy started crying in happiness. Sebastian took her hand and Kevin took Beattie's hand. They were all smiling.

"Walk through the mist that you are seeing," said the angel, "and know that you are home."

They all turned to watch the angel as she flew up and disappeared into what seemed to be the peacock-blue sky of the painting. The mist was clearing and they skipped, together, into it with feet so light that they felt as though they were flying. When the mist was gone, they all saw that they were back in Tracy's bedroom, her real bedroom at the castle, and the painting was just a picture on the wall.

They all turned and looked at each other in great happiness. They hugged Beattie.

"You're amazing. You've rescued us all, Beattie," said Sebastian. "Thank goodness you were here." Beattie beamed with pleasure and gazed at Sebastian.

"I was so afraid," she said modestly.

"But you were so brave," said Tracy.

"So were all of you," said Beattie. "It's all thanks to this wonderful silver, heart-shaped locket that

Aunt Alice gave me. She said it once belonged to her mother who was also called Beatrice like me, and that is why she gave it to me."

"This has taken the whole night," said Kevin. "Look, it's dawn. Let's go out into the garden and watch the sun rising."

Tracy, who was in her nightdress, went into the bathroom to get dressed into some warm clothes, and the others put their jackets on. They had forgotten to take them with them into the picture, but Beattie and Kevin had brought their jackets with them when coming from the cottage the night before. They were lying on a chair in Tracy's room. Sebastian went into his room to fetch his, and came back again. When they were all ready, they opened Tracy's bedroom door and made their way along the corridor quietly, so as not to awaken Aunt Alice. Silently they climbed down the stairs and made their way out into the garden. There was a beautiful sunrise. It was going to be a beautiful, sunny day. They sat on a bench and watched the sun coming up over the mountains in silence. How wonderful it was to be free; to be back in their own world again.

"What are we going to say happened to you, Tracy?" asked Beattie. "They will ask where you were."

"I think we'll have to tell the truth and say I was spirited away," said Tracy.

"But who by?" asked Kevin.

"Evil magic," said Tracy. "It's true."

"How are they ever going to believe it?" said Sebastian.

"I don't know, but you can show them the secret passage and the chamber with all the witches' books," said Tracy, "and they can go up there and find all those magical things. Then they will have to believe it."

Kevin looked doubtful. "Anyway, Dad will be amazed that we have found a secret passage in the cellar," he said.

"The only sad thing is that we didn't find any treasure," said Sebastian. "We found the secret chamber, but there was no treasure hidden there. That was the whole reason we were searching for the chamber, wasn't it? It was just a room of witchcraft after all, full of terrifying dark magic."

"Well, at least we're safe," said Beattie. They all nodded.

The four of them sat on the bench in the garden watching the sun come up for quite a while. When it was getting on for a quarter to seven, Kevin and Beattie got up to go back to their cottage; they remembered that their mother would be up and about soon.

Tracy and Sebastian stood up too, but suddenly Tracy turned pale. She fainted and fell to the wet ground in a puddle of water. The others tried in vain to get her to stand on her feet.

"Oh, poor Tracy," gasped Beattie. "She's exhausted. She has not had anything to eat or drink since the day before yesterday, has she?"

"I don't think we needed food in that ghostly world of the picture," said Sebastian, "but of course, this has been a terribly frightening ordeal for her, worse than it was for all of us, as she was in there longer."

They could not get Tracy to stand up – she had collapsed and was now soaking wet. Sebastian and Kevin picked her up between them, with the intention of carrying her back to the castle to put her to bed. Suddenly Marjorie appeared out of her cottage door and saw them.

"Tracy, oh Tracy," she shouted out in delight. "You have found her! How wonderful. But is she all right? Is she unconscious?"

"She's fainted," said Kevin.

"Oh, let's get her to bed quickly," cried Marjorie. "She must be ill. She has been missing for a whole day and night in that terrible rainfall and storm. She's so wet. We must take care of her."

The boys carried Tracy upstairs and carefully lowered her onto her bed. Tracy looked as though she were asleep. Marjorie stripped off some of her wet clothes and covered her with a blanket. She put her hand on Tracy's forehead. "She has a high temperature," she said.

Tracy stirred and opened her eyes a little. "I was spirited away by something terrible," she murmured. "I was trapped, I could not get out."

"She is delirious," said Marjorie. "She must have got lost somewhere, and all that torrential rain and the damp and cold has made her delirious. She must rest and not try to speak."

It did look as though Tracy was delirious. She started murmuring in an unintelligible way.

"This has all been too much for her," said Sebastian when Marjorie had gone out of the room to get a hot-water bottle and some more blankets. "She really has fainted. She does need to rest."

Marjorie came back with the hot-water bottle and the blankets. "Now I want you all to leave her alone to sleep," said Marjorie. "Thank goodness she is safely home. I think she does not realise how terrible the weather can be up here and how quickly it can change. She has never been to the Highlands of Scotland before, has she, Sebastian?"

"No," said Sebastian. "Neither of us has."

"So, we'll all go down to breakfast now," said Marjorie. "Aunt Alice will be down in a few minutes and we can tell her the good news – that Tracy is back and resting in her room. Aunt Alice will be so relieved."

Aunt Alice was relieved. "Oh, thank goodness," she said when she heard the news. "I am sure she did not realise just how easy it is to get lost in the forest up here. It happened before, years ago, at my second cousin's twenty-first birthday party here in the castle, that a couple were lost for two days and could not find their way back. There are so many paths, and the forest goes on for miles. We had to call out a search party. Luckily it was summer and not raining, but everybody was terribly upset about it. There is not much to eat in the forest either except a few blueberries and raspberries. They drank water from a stream."

"When she has had a good sleep and wakes up, I will take some hot soup up for her and try to coax her to eat," said Marjorie. "If we had electricity we could ask a doctor to call, but of course we can't do that. We will see how she is tomorrow, and tonight Wilfred will be back."

"I expect in town they will know about the electric wires being down," said Aunt Alice. "We have had the wires down before. I expect the electricity company will send somebody to repair them soon."

After breakfast they all went up to have a look at Tracy and sat with her for a while. She slept for the whole day, and was not even able to drink the hot soup that Marjorie brought up for her. Marjorie filled up the hot-water bottle again for her, and left her to sleep. It was not until Wilfred came back in the early evening, that Tracy began to stir.

Chapter Fifteen

A CELEBRATION

As Wilfred entered the house, Kevin ran up to him immediately to tell him about the secret passage they had discovered in the cellar. Wilfred stared at him in surprise. He certainly had not known that it existed.

"Tomorrow I'll be exploring that," said Wilfred excitedly. "Have you told Aunt Alice yet?"

"Not yet," said Kevin, and then he told Wilfred about Tracy. How she had been missing for a whole day and was now resting upstairs.

They all, except Tracy, sat down to dinner in the big dining room. Wilfred told them that in town, the electric company did know that the electric wires were down, and they would be sending someone to repair them tomorrow. He said how difficult it had been driving back along waterlogged roads, but his van had very good wheels suited to extreme weather conditions in the Highlands.

Sebastian then told the adults about the ancient book of estate plans he had found in the hidden cavity on the top shelf of the library. He told them about the secret passage they had found in the cellar. Kevin carried on with the story and recounted how they had gone up it and discovered that it led to a secret chamber next to one of the towers. Beattie told them about the books of magic and objects of witchcraft that they had found there.

Marjorie was horrified. "So that is what you were doing down in the cellar," she said. "The local legends about witchcraft happening in this castle were right, then. That's horrible."

Aunt Alice was amazed. "So the secret chamber exists after all!" she said. "What a surprise! And you found a secret passage as well! How wonderful that after all these years you four have managed to discover them."

"But there is no treasure in the secret chamber," said Beattie sadly. "It's very disappointing. We searched the room. There are horrible old ornaments of devils and witches in there and a cauldron as well as books of magic spells."

"Tracy must have run off because the idea of it terrified her," said Marjorie to Sebastian. "That's why I didn't want you and Tracy to know about the legends of witchcraft that took place here long ago. I was sure that it would give you nightmares and spoil your holiday."

"Yes," said Sebastian, "but I think we would have

found out about it sooner or later, just from legends of the castle that are recorded in modern books."

"Yes, most certainly you would have," sighed Aunt Alice. "Now we just have to concentrate on getting Tracy back on her feet."

Later that evening when they were all standing around Tracy's bed, she opened her eyes and smiled.

"How are you, dear?" asked Aunt Alice. "Try her with the soup again now, will you Marjorie?"

Tracy sat up in bed with pillows to support her and drank some of the soup. "I really was spirited away," she said. "You will never believe me, but I found myself outside the castle and then I got trapped in that picture on the wall – that beautiful painting there. I could not get out for a whole day. We were rescued by an angel."

Wilfred laughed. Marjorie looked at him. "She has been delirious for hours," she said. "She fell unconscious in the grounds of the castle, and Kevin and Sebastian carried her in, early in the morning. We put her to bed."

"She has, I am certain, been wandering lost in the forest," said Aunt Alice, "You mustn't be frightened anymore, Tracy, dear. You've been having horrid nightmares. They are not real. You are safe now."

"I'm not afraid anymore," said Tracy. "I saw the most beautiful angel, and she rescued us and blessed the painting. She came to us in the painting and there's no dark spell on it anymore."

"Of course there isn't," said Aunt Alice. " I have never seen that painting of the castle before. It has never been up on the wall here as far as I remember. Where did you find it Marjorie?"

"In one of the spare rooms upstairs, hidden in a panel in the bottom of an old wardrobe," said Marjorie. "As I was searching for things with which to decorate Sebastian's and Tracy's rooms, the bottom of the wardrobe unexpectedly slid away in my hand. I must have pressed something inside the wardrobe that was keeping the painting hidden there."

"What wonderful discoveries we have made in just a few days since you children came here," said Aunt Alice.

The next morning, after breakfast, Kevin, Beattie and Sebastian took Wilfred down into the cellar. They took their torches and squeezed along the narrow passageway. Wilfred stepped from the passage into the chamber first. He was amazed to see all the articles of witchcraft in the room.

"I'm going to knock a hole in the wall, with Aunt Alice's permission," said Wilfred when they were standing inside the dusty chamber. "I know she would like to see all these things, and it would be too difficult bringing them up the passage.

Obviously they were brought down here once, but that was a long time ago."

★

The next morning, when the electric power was back and Wilfred's powerful electric tools could be used, Sebastian, Kevin and Beattie went up into the tower with him to help him break the wall. They knew exactly which place in the tower concealed the secret chamber, and were able to knock some of the stones out to create a gap large enough for them to step through into the secret chamber behind. It was so much easier than going up the secret passage in the cellar.

Aunt Alice and Marjorie both climbed the tower stairs to come up and see the chamber. They peered through the gap and stared at the articles of witchcraft. They were astounded.

"We must phone the museum in Inverness," said Aunt Alice, "and ask them to send some curators to look at all these things here. They might have some historical value for the museum."

"There is no feeling at all of anything sinister about these ornaments now, is there?" whispered Kevin to Sebastian, looking at the ugly figurines of devils, ogres and witches lying around on the floor.

"No, the spell has been completely broken,"

whispered back Sebastian. "You can feel it. There is nothing bad at all about the atmosphere in this chamber any more. Those evil creatures are dead even in their spirit world. They have been destroyed forever in this castle."

"How absurd," said Aunt Alice, looking through the gap at the devilish ornaments, "that the first Duke's son should play with objects like these and imagine that they had magical powers that could destroy the castle. Wherever did he get them from? No wonder he went crazy. How very silly it all is."

★

In the afternoon, Wilfred made some phone calls for Aunt Alice, and the next day, curators from the museum in Inverness made the journey out to the castle to examine all the articles in the secret chamber. They brought with them an expert who would be able to value them.

The curators spent a long time in the secret chamber looking at everything. They brought special cloths with them to wipe the dust off the objects. After about an hour, they came out and asked Aunt Alice and her housekeeper and caretaker if they would be kind enough to come and sit in the lounge on the ground floor. They said they had some important news to impart to Aunt Alice about the articles in the chamber.

The three adults went into the lounge and made themselves comfortable there. They waited in anticipation. Sebastian, Kevin, Beattie and Tracy also followed them in there out of curiosity. Tracy was feeling much better now.

"Perhaps the Curators will ask Aunt Alice to give everything to their museum," said Kevin.

"Good riddance to everything in the chamber of witchcraft," said Beattie. "Those horrible creatures are all dead ornaments now – stone dead! But I will be glad to see the back of them."

"So will I," said Tracy. "I hope they take them all away."

The curators entered the room, and one of the men stood up and addressed Aunt Alice, as the owner of the castle. He shook hands with her.

"Madam, I have asked you to sit down in here because what I am about to say to you, may be a matter of tremendous surprise and even shock to you."

He went on, "I congratulate you for having discovered in this secret chamber, in Creag Castle, these amazing historical art treasures. All of them are at least four hundred years old and they have a value which is absolutely priceless. Not only do they have great historical value, but the materials of which these figurines are made are worth a fortune in themselves – gold, silver, jade, coral and amber are some of the materials used, with diamonds, rubies and emeralds for their eyes." He held up two of the statues: a witch and a vampire-like creature which he had brought down from the chamber. "These are made of jade and amber with gold, and look at the rubies in their eyes! Look how they shine!

"The table is an amazing vintage antique – it is mahogany inlaid with rare mother of pearl. The books are so old and rare – each of them is worth thousands of pounds.

"If you wish to sell even a few pieces, Madam, you will be a very rich woman."

There was a stunned silence in the room as everybody took in the news. Marjorie went over to hold Aunt Alice's hand. Aunt Alice was staring in amazement at the man who was speaking. She looked as though she was struck dumb.

Suddenly she started laughing joyously. "This is the treasure, obviously! This is it! You children have found it! You have saved the castle for me! How absolutely wonderful!"

Everybody in the room cheered, including Wilfred. Beattie started dancing around the room. Tracy went over to Aunt Alice and put her arms around her.

"I am so happy," she said. "I am so glad we have

found the treasure for you. I can hardly believe it. Now you can always stay in the castle, and we can visit you here."

Sebastian clapped his hands, "All the things in the secret chamber were covered in such thick dust, and it was dark in there. We never realised that anything was made of gold or jewels," he said.

"Yes, everything looked dirty and horrible looking," said Kevin. "We never dreamed we had found the treasure!"

"We were just concerned with the magic and rescuing Tracy, weren't we?" whispered Beattie to her brother and Sebastian.

"They'll never know what we went through," said Sebastian quietly. "Our lives are more valuable than any treasure."

"You are right," said Aunt Alice, hearing the last part of what Sebastian had just said. "You children are so clever and wise, far beyond your ages."

"We are all wiser than we were a few days ago," said Tracy.

"Yes, we are wise enough to keep away from bewitched pictures and passages under the ground," whispered Kevin.

Beattie giggled. The other three turned away to hide their smiles.

"How amazing it has all been," said Sebastian. They all nodded.

Marjorie went out into the kitchen to make them all a cup of tea, and the curators looked at the painting of the castle in Tracy's room. They declared it also to be valuable since it was so old and had been painted by the Duke who had built the castle, so long ago.

"I am going to donate that painting to the museum," said Aunt Alice.

"It's been blessed by an angel. We saw it fly into the sky of the picture," said Tracy. The curators smiled.

Tracy knew the adults would not believe her, but it didn't seem to matter any more. Everything felt like a fairy tale now anyway.

That evening there was a phone call from Spain. Mr and Mrs Stewart were coming back home from their holiday the following week and said they would like to come up to Creag Castle for the weekend, to see the castle for the last time.

Tracy giggled. "Let's not tell them about the treasure yet," she said. "Let's wait until they get here and then spring it on them as a surprise!"

The next few days passed like a dream. Aunt Alice wrote out a huge shopping list, and Wilfred and Marjorie went into town buying up all the good things they could find for a feast. Finally, when Tracy's and Sebastian's parents arrived at the castle, Aunt Alice had everything ready for a celebration.

Nobody said a word to them about the treasure

until everyone was sitting at the table ready to eat. Aunt Alice opened a bottle of champagne. "We are all going to have some," she said. "Nobody is too young or too old to drink champagne at my table today."

She stood up to get everybody's attention and looked especially at Mr and Mrs Stewart.

"I have an announcement to make," she said. "Thanks to these wonderful young people here, I shall no longer have to sell this beautiful castle. I can stay here as long as I please, and you as my nearest relatives, will inherit it when I leave this earth."

Mr and Mrs Stewart stared at her in surprise.

Aunt Alice raised her glass in the air and smiled at everybody.

"We have found the secret chamber and the treasure," shouted Sebastian. "Hooray!"

He raised his glass in the air too, and his parents gasped loudly. Everybody cheered.

At that moment, Aunt Alice happened to look across at Beattie. "Is that necklace you are wearing the one I gave you for your birthday last year, dear?" she asked.

"Yes, it is," said Beattie.

"I'm so glad you like it," said Aunt Alice.

"Oh, yes, I love it," replied Beattie, ecstatically. "I'm always going to wear it. Thank you so much Aunt Alice."

Aunt Alice beamed at her and so did Marjorie.

"Little do they really know," whispered Sebastian.

"And now I know angels really do exist," said Tracy.